HANNAH AND THE MAGIC EYE

HANNAH
AND THE
MAGIC EYE

Tyler Enfield

A NOVEL

GREAT PLAINS
TEEN FICTION

Great Plains Publications
233 Garfield Street
Winnipeg, MB R3G 2MI
www.greatplains.mb.ca

Great Plains Publications gratefully acknowledges the financial support
provided for its publishing program by the Government of Canada through
the Canada Book Fund; the Canada Council for the Arts; the Province of
Manitoba through the Book Publishing Tax Credit and the Book Publisher
Marketing Assistance Program; and the Manitoba Arts Council.

Design & Typography by Relish New Brand Experience
Printed in Canada by Friesens
Second printing 2017

LIBRARY AND ARCHIVES CANADA CATALOGUING IN PUBLICATION

Enfield, Tyler, author
    Hannah and the magic eye / Tyler Enfield.

Issued in print and electronic formats.
ISBN 978-1-927855-68-3 (softcover).--ISBN 978-1-927855-69-0 (EPUB).--
ISBN 978-1-927855-70-6 (Kindle)

    1. Title.

PS8609.N4H36 2017   JC813'.6   C2017-900065-9
                                         C2017-900066-7

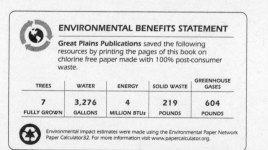

ENVIRONMENTAL BENEFITS STATEMENT

Great Plains Publications saved the following
resources by printing the pages of this book on
chlorine free paper made with 100% post-consumer
waste.

TREES	WATER	ENERGY	SOLID WASTE	GREENHOUSE GASES
7	3,276	4	219	604
FULLY GROWN	GALLONS	MILLION BTUs	POUNDS	POUNDS

Environmental impact estimates were made using the Environmental Paper Network
Paper Calculator 3.2. For more information visit www.papercalculator.org.

Canada

FSC
www.fsc.org
MIX
Paper from
responsible sources
FSC™ C016245

For Indigo, my fellow adventurer...

Hannah Dubuisson sat alone on the airplane. She was twelve years old. She wore a printed summer dress, patent leather shoes, and she was very, very, excited.

Her plane ticket read:

> Aegean Flight 451
> Departing: Brussels, Belgium 9:28 am
> Arriving: Tel Aviv, Israel 3:07 pm

Her mind raced, imagining the adventures awaiting her below.

Hannah gazed out the window, snapping photos of clouds. She flipped through complimentary magazines. She accepted the pretzels and soft drinks and little packets of handwipes. Anything and everything the stewardess offered, Hannah placed upon her tray, stacking it neatly. Hannah's only thought was for her final destination.

Jerusalem.

She could not wait.

"Pretzels?" offered the stewardess, pushing her enormous trolley down the narrow aisle.

"Merci," said Hannah, receiving the small, crinkly, silver bag and carefully arranging it with her other in-flight souvenirs.

Thinking of what lay ahead in Jerusalem, Hannah felt a thrill of anticipation. She had spent the last four summers helping her grandfather, the famed archaeologist Henri Dubuisson, in his various excavations around Jerusalem. Hannah was passionate about archaeology, and she waited all year for these expeditions.

"Coca cola?" said the stewardess, holding a bright red can aloft.

"Merci," replied Hannah, balancing the can atop a first, which had yet to be opened.

A bell chimed overhead. The captain's voice announced first in French, then in Hebrew, and finally in English, that they were encountering some turbulence, and the ride might get bumpy. Hannah's Hebrew was rusty, but she understood all three languages, and noted the differences in phrasing.

The "fasten your seatbelt" light lit up overhead. The plane jounced about, and Hannah secured her seatbelt. Other passengers did the same. Hannah shoved the camera into her red backpack, trading it out for the book lying at the bottom. She held the book in her lap, glancing at its cover. It was called *An Illustrated Guidebook To Israel's Historic Sites*. It had turned up in the postbox last week, addressed to Hannah in Brussels. Grandpa Henri must have sent it so she could brush up on her history before the visit.

There was nothing unusual about the book itself. Henri often sent books, and they were always about history, or archaeology, or ancient symbols and ciphers. There was just one thing about the book that struck Hannah as odd. Henri had included a message, written on a blue sticky-note, pressed to the first page.

It said:

1. Keep the map safe
2. Beware the *Cancellarii*
–
–
5. Remember, Hannah, you have the magic eye!

Hannah looked at this note now. Here's what she understood:

None of it.

Grandpa Henri always said archaeologists are like detectives. They hunt for clues and try to put them together in a way that tells a story about the people who left them. If it weren't for archaeologists, we would understand nothing of the ancient people who built the pyramids of Egypt, or chipped out arrowheads in America, or painted on the walls of French caves.

Needless to say, Hannah was intrigued. First of all, she knew nothing about a map. Second, she had never heard of the Cancellarii. Third, what happened to numbers 3 and 4 on the list? They must be important. And last of all, what in the world was a magic eye?

Hannah was like a puppy with a piece of gum: she had no idea what she'd come into, but it was tremendously interesting and she had no intention of putting it down. It was just like Henri to spark her interest in some new mystery prior to her arrival. Perhaps this was his way of teasing her.

"Please return your seats to their upright positions," said the stewardess over the intercom. "Secure your trays to the seatback before you. We are now preparing to land."

Hannah shut the book. She placed it flat at the bottom of her backpack, forming a nice, neat platform for her compass, her camera, her phone, and her collapsible red umbrella. She liked to be organized. Henri always said the main difference between an archaeologist and a grave-robber was a person's desire to share history, rather than plunder it, and this could only be accomplished with the proper organization of a dig site. Organization. You had to be organized.

Plus, now Hannah had plenty of room for her in-flight snacks and drinks.

When Henri didn't arrive to meet her at Ben Gurion Airport's luggage carousel, Hannah wasn't worried. Henri was often late, caught up at a dig site, enraptured by some find and completely unaware of the time. So Hannah stood with the other passengers by the carousel, waiting for her luggage.

The passengers were from every part of the world. She saw orthodox Jews in their dour black suits, Greek orthodox priests with huge fuzzy hats, Palestinian women in hijabs, Filipino nuns, African businessmen, young backpackers,

Saudis with keffiyeh, and just about everywhere you looked, Israeli soldiers, police, and security guards with machine guns, eyeing everyone and everything that moved through this airport.

The carousel's conveyor belt lurched along, and every few moments someone came and yanked their suitcase away. Soon Hannah saw her vintage red suitcase approaching. It had a leather strap up the front and a brass buckle near the top. She grabbed the handle and tugged at it, but the suitcase was heavy and stubbornly dragged her about the carousel until she managed to haul it from the belt.

Once she got it on wheels, her suitcase was better behaved. Hannah rolled it through the glass doors, exiting Ben Gurion Airport. She stood on the curb, scanning the cars for Henri's beat up Peugeot. She saw a white limousine pull up. That would never be him. She saw shuttles idling in the parking lot, taxicabs jostling for the curb.

But where was Henri?

Hannah glanced at the people around her. She checked her watch. Then her cellphone. There was no message from Henri. She tried dialing him, but there was no answer. She left a message and hung up.

She was about to return the cellphone to her backpack when the phone's wallpaper caught her eye. This happened often. The wallpaper was a picture of her herself, five years old, sitting on her father's lap in the kitchen. A hazy, scenic light streamed through the window by the table. Her father was drinking a cup of coffee and reading a book—but not to her, it was an adult book—while she happily smiled for the camera. She had only one front tooth in the photograph, and it was a silly photograph and her only reason for keeping it was because it was the last one. The very last photograph ever taken of Hannah and her father together.

She lifted the phone to dial Henri again and paused. Across the parking lot was a young Palestinian Arab straddling a parked motorcycle. He wore blue jeans, a white tank top, dark sunglasses, and a gold chain around his neck. And he was watching her. He made no attempt to hide it. When the young man met Hannah's eye, he removed a cellphone from his pocket and called someone, all the while staring directly at Hannah.

Still standing on the airport's curb, a nervous twinge grabbed at her gut. Her palms went moist. She again searched for Henri's car, more desperately this time. She checked her watch. When she looked up, the man on the motorcycle was still watching her, still talking on the cell phone.

A minute later a black sedan with tinted windows pulled alongside the young Palestinian. He leaned in to speak with whomever was in the backseat. Hannah saw a woman's hand emerge from the window and point in Hannah's direction. The sedan screeched away and the young Palestinian started his motorcycle. He rode slowly toward Hannah.

She gasped and spun around. With her heart thumping in her chest, Hannah began wheeling her suitcase along the pavement in the opposite direction. The young man came up beside her on his motorcycle. He kept pace as she walked. Just putting along, only a few feet away. Hannah refused to look at him. She could smell the exhaust from his bike. But she was running out of sidewalk, and would soon be leaving the airport proper, along with the safety of the crowds. She had to think of something fast.

A taxicab approached from the opposite lane. She had no time to lose. She jumped the curb, cutting directly before the motorcyclist as she crossed the street and stood in the path of the approaching cab, waving her arms until it halted before her. Without speaking to the driver she jumped into the backseat and hauled the red suitcase in after.

"Jerusalem," she said. "Take me to Jerusalem."

The cab driver studied her in the rearview mirror. "How old are you? Where are your parents?" he asked in English.

"Take me to Jerusalem now," she replied in Hebrew.

He seemed reluctant. "You have money?"

"Plenty," she replied. "Go. Just go."

"Not till I know where you're going. Jerusalem's a big city."

"Just go! To the Old City! Go! Go!"

The motorcyclist sat astride his bike, not five feet away, calmly appraising them through his dark sunglasses. But the cab driver wasn't leaving till he had a proper destination. "The Old City has eleven gates." He began counting on his fingers. "You got Jaffa Gate. You got Herod's Gate. You got Lion's Gate. You got—"

"That one!" she shouted, having no real idea which gate was nearest Henri's home. "Take me to that one."

"Lion's Gate?"

"Yes."

The driver glanced at her once more in the mirror, put the car in gear, and drove away.

"All right. Lion's Gate it is."

It was usually a forty-minute drive from Ben Gurion Airport to Henri's home in the Jewish Quarter of the Old City of Jerusalem. But it was now just after 4pm, and if evening traffic was any slower they'd be parked. Hannah glanced out the back window of the cab. There was the young Palestinian, practically glued to the bumper.

With painstaking effort, Hannah's cab inched into the next lane. She glanced behind her again, just as the motorcyclist switched lanes, staying as close as possible. He gave Hannah a grim smile and she spun back around, clutching the fabric of her seat.

This cannot be happening. This cannot be happening. Why was this happening? Hannah was a just a child, alone in a foreign country, and someone bad was actually, really, following her. This was not a movie. This was for real.

A few minutes later, the cab halted at a traffic light. The motorcyclist pulled alongside Hannah's window, waiting for the green light. He revved the motor to get her attention. Hannah told herself not to look. No matter what, do not look at this man. Do not look.

She looked.

He was inches away, staring directly at her. He reached out and rapped on the window twice with his knuckles—clack, clack—and then the light turned green and the cab pulled away.

"You know that guy?" asked the driver, turning left onto the two-lane highway to Jerusalem.

Hannah shook her head.

"He seems to know you."

"Please drive."

"Do you see me doing something else?"

Hannah removed her phone and dialed Henri again. This time she got nothing. His phone was completely disconnected. A ball of panic tightened in her throat. She fought it back, forcing herself to concentrate. To think.

Hannah tried to recall the layout of the Old City. She should have a plan before she exited the taxi. Some kind of route in mind.

Old Jerusalem and new Jerusalem were basically two separate cities. The first was tucked within the second like a nucleus within a cell, completely walled off by ancient limestone ramparts. While new Jerusalem was a metropolis of modern buildings and traffic lights and shopping malls, the Old City was a gigantic fort atop a hill, built three thousand years ago by King Solomon. Stepping into the Old City was like stepping back in time—a storybook wonderland filled with carpet sellers and camels and cramped little alleys that looked like something from the adventures of Aladdin.

Using her cell phone again, Hannah did an internet search for the Lion's Gate. Looking at the image, she saw cars going in and out. Two lanes of traffic. Which meant whoever was behind her would have no trouble following directly into the Old City.

She did an image search for the other gates. One of them, Damascus Gate, had no entry for vehicles. It was for pedestrians only. Also, there was a busy market out front, which meant crowds, which meant chaos, which meant she just might be able to sneak into the city without the motorcyclist following behind.

"Take me to Damascus Gate," she said, redirecting the driver.

"You said Lion's Gate."

"Yes, and now I am saying Damascus Gate."

He glanced in the mirror. "Your money. Your call."

Hannah knew once she was safely through Damascus gate, she would be entering one of the most confusing mazes on earth—the Muslim Quarter of old Jerusalem—and finding her way to the Jewish Quarter would be a medieval adventure in itself.

The cab left the highway, entering the outskirts of Jerusalem. The Old City and its enormous walls would be visible soon, high atop the hill called Mount Moriah.

"How much farther?" asked Hannah, glancing over her shoulder. The motorcyclist was now two cars behind and working to catch up.

"In this traffic?" replied the driver. "Fifteen minutes. Maybe twenty. You sure you got money?"

"I told you I did. Please do not ask again."

Uncertain what to do, Hannah unzipped her backpack and dug out her copy of *An Illustrated Guidebook To Israel's Historic Sites*. She opened the front cover, and reread the note from Henri. He was trying to warn her, that much was clear. Did the Cancellarii have something to do with Henri's absence, and this young Palestinian on the motorcycle? Hannah sensed that if she could solve the riddle of the note, she might be able to find some way out of this mess.

She read it again.

1. Keep the map safe
2. Beware the *Cancellarii*
   —
   —
5. Remember, Hannah, you have the magic eye!

Why hadn't Henri written numbers 3 and 4 on the list? More than ever, it seemed he was hinting at something. But what?

On impulse, Hannah opened the book to page three. The page was missing. Page four on the backside was missing too. It wasn't torn from the book, but carefully cut out, which explained why she hadn't noticed before. So the missing numbers on the list were simply to draw her attention to a page that wasn't there. Again, she wondered why.

Using her phone, she did an internet search. It was crazy, but so was this situation, so there was no harm in trying. Into the browser she typed:

Henri Dubuisson, where are pages 3 and 4?

The browser brought back numerous hits, everything that included Henri's name. But the website at the very top of the page, the one that matched her search exactly, was titled *My Dearest Hannah*. And it was authored by her grandfather. Hannah clicked on the link. She was taken to a solitary page. It was completely white.

At first she thought there was no writing on the page, but then she remembered the trick. Henri had taught it to her. She clicked the upper corner of the white page and dragged the cursor down to the bottom until the whole page was highlighted blue. Suddenly visible against the blue, she could now see white lettering. Henri had written in white upon the page's white background, and the letters could only be seen when highlighted. Here is what Hannah saw:

USERNAME: _____

PASSWORD: _____

There was nothing else on the page. Realizing Henri had created this webpage for her alone, she entered her own name as the username. She typed, *Hannah Dubuisson*.

But what about the password? Was there some word that had a special meaning for both of them? Of course!

Baklava, she typed. It was her favorite desert, and a running joke between them because Henri could not stand the stuff, complaining the honey-drizzled pastries made his bushy white mustache too sticky. *Baklava*, it turned out, was also the password to the page Henri had created for Hannah's eyes only.

She was taken to another webpage, which was essentially a private letter written from Henri to her.

My dearest Hannah,
If you are reading this now, it is because you truly are a Dubuisson, and therefore clever as fox—I salute you! Unfortunately, it also means things have gone horribly wrong. This letter exists as a Plan B, if you will, to be activated only in the direst of circumstances. That you are reading it now means I have already sent you the guidebook with its clues, and therefore, my dear, we are both in grave danger.

Read this letter closely. Our lives may now depend upon its instructions. I am counting on you.

For the next several moments Hannah sat very still in the back of the cab, her heart pounding like a drum. Only when her breathing slowed was she able to continue reading the letter.

As you know, for the last several years I have conducted numerous archeological digs throughout Israel. The university has paid me well and covered the excavation costs. My real reason for remaining in Jerusalem, however, has been to continue my search for a most significant treasure. A treasure beyond your wildest dreams, Hannah. Locating this treasure has been my life's work.

But I am not alone in my search. A very old and very powerful secret society of treasure hunters is searching too. They are called the Cancellarii, and they will stop at nothing to find it. For years they have tried to uncover the hiding place of my secret map, and I fear they may at last be close.

Do not underestimate the Cancellarii, Hannah. They are smart, determined, and dangerous. It is entirely possible this letter is already in their hands. For this reason, I have not placed all my instructions in one location, but have instead spread them out, ensuring their safety.

Hannah, I need you to retrieve the treasure map and keep it safe from the Cancellarii. I have already given you the tools you need. You are my clever little fox.

Find it.

Hannah sat there, stunned, with the phone in her hand. She looked out the window. In the distance, she saw the enormous stone walls surrounding the Old City, and the domes of its churches, synagogues, and mosques rising above.

Hannah had asked for an adventure, and now here it was, burning like a coal in her lap. A secret society called the Cancellarii was after her. She was meant to search for a treasure map and keep it hidden for Henri. And though he insisted Hannah had everything she needed, she had no idea where to begin.

More than ever, she had to find him. Only Henri could explain what to do with the map. Only Henri would know how to deal with the Cancellarii.

Please Henri, she thought. *Please be safe at home.*

"Almost there," said the cabbie. "But I won't be able to park beside Damascus Gate. Too many people right now."

From the side pocket in her backpack, Hannah removed her 'emergency fund' and counted out money for the fare. The moment the cab stopped she flung the money onto the front seat, jumped out the back door and bolted into the crowd, wheeling her red suitcase behind. She checked her shoulder and saw the young Palestinian idling his motorcycle by the curb, attempting to park, but a traffic officer waved him along. The young man fixed Hannah with his eyes, and the two stared for an instant. The traffic officer began blowing his whistle. The motorcyclist gunned his engine, glanced at Hannah one last time, and sped away.

Hannah hurried over the polished cobbles leading to Damascus Gate, her suitcase clunk-clunking along. As she passed beneath its enormous limestone arch and entered the Old City proper, she suddenly halted. Hannah gazed about her, turning in place.

She was here. In the ancient city of Jerusalem.

The Muslim Quarter was a mindbending labyrinth of dark twisting alleys and cool shaded cafés and yellow birds chirping from rusty old cages. She smelled frankincense, its gray smoke floating like ghosts through the marketplace. Dogs barked. Children hollered. Bells jangled on the handles of nut carts and date carts. The alleys were crammed with wet boxes of vegetables and tables of T-shirts, plastic combs from Taiwan and stacks of CDs, enormous burlap sacks filled with coffee beans and lentils and old men reading newspapers amidst clouds of cigarette smoke and women hanging laundry on rooftops and TVs blaring from every window, shop, restaurant, and home.

It was a dizzying carnival for the senses. Hannah was barely ten feet inside the city, and already she was lost. Just this morning Hannah had waved goodbye to her mother in Belgium. Now here she was, a young Jewish girl with a backpack and a red suitcase in hand, standing alone in the Muslim Quarter of the Old City of Jerusalem—one of the most exotic places on earth.

Somewhere in this chaos was a path to Henri's home in the Jewish Quarter. But Hannah had no idea how to find it. She looked about for a friendly face. None jumped out. The truth was, she was a Jew in an Arab neighborhood, and there was little love between the Palestinian Arabs and the Jews of this town. It had been this way for more than half a century. Each culture had their own separate area within Jerusalem to protect their holy places. Same for the Armenians, and the Greeks, and the Moroccans, and the Russians and the... come to think of it, since Jerusalem was considered a holy city to all three major religions—Judaism, Christianity, and Islam—nearly every nation on Earth had some special nook in this city, reserved for their unique form of worship.

And yet even with all those different cultures and languages and beliefs and races, all of them brushing shoulders in the narrow alleys of Jerusalem, none got along worse than the Palestinian Arabs and the Israeli Jews. For this reason, Hannah thought it best to leave her Hebrew behind and speak in English or French on this side of town.

She approached a man selling olives on a rickety table. There were green olives and black olives and purple olives, olives in jars and olives in boxes and heaps of olives floating in buckets of oil. "Which way to the Jewish Quarter?" she asked in French.

The man spit an olive pit into his hand and let it drop. Without looking at her, he jabbed his thumb in the direction of a nearby alley.

Hannah wheeled her suitcase over the flagstones, the alley cool and smoky beneath the shade of awnings. A dog skulked past, and two boys sprinted after. Arabic pop music blared from a window overhead. The alley opened onto a small plaza. Hannah saw café tables with men playing backgammon. Children kicked a soccer ball against a wall that was, she realized, probably twice as old as Belgium. Her path didn't continue straight, but split into several more alleys, each leading from the plaza. There was also a set of stone stairs leading up to… a home? A mosque? A distant ringed planet? Anything seemed possible.

Leaning against a nearby wall, three Palestinian boys shared a single cigarette, passing it between them. As they talked, they kept glancing her way. They were perhaps sixteen years old. She could smell their cologne. One boy tossed the cigarette and squashed it beneath his shoe. He approached Hannah with a smile.

"You are lost?" he said in Hebrew.

She nodded.

"You need a guide?"

"That depends," she said in English, glancing left and right down the alley. "What is your fee for guiding me to the Jewish Quarter?"

"For you?" he said. "Very good price. A good deal for you. I am the very best guide."

"How much?" she repeated, gripping her suitcase's handle with both hands.

"How much you want to pay?" he said, opening his arms in a gesture of generosity.

Lost she may be, but Hannah was no fool. There would be no generosity coming from this one, with his oily smile and stink of cologne, his frequent glances at her grip on the suitcase.

"I will find my own way, thank you," she said.

"Come on!" he insisted. "You did not even say how much. How much you want to pay? I will take you! I know Jerusalem!"

Before Hannah could respond, another Palestinian boy suddenly appeared between them. He argued with the first in rapid-fire Arabic. It sounded like a squabble.

This newcomer was half the size of the first and considerably younger, though he stood his ground like a lion. Hannah had no idea what he was saying, but he was saying it loudly and fiercely, and the older boy was backing up, eventually rejoining his friends with a look of sheepish defiance.

This new boy, who stood six inches shorter than Hannah, took her confidently by the arm and led her toward a coffee stall on the other side of the plaza. "Forget them," he said. "They are gangsters. You know gangsters?"

Hannah nodded.

"Gangsters," he repeated, mimicking two pistols being fired. "There are too many in Jerusalem."

This new boy wore a blue, American style T-shirt. He wore American style sunglasses that were too big for his face. He said he was eighteen, though he appeared younger than Hannah.

"You like coffee?" he asked.

She nodded.

"My family makes the very best coffee. Please, sit." The boy proudly pushed his uncle aside and began portioning out coffee grounds. Pouring the water. Setting it all to boil. It was a very basic coffee stall. It had a charcoal burner, a few cups, and a soapy bucket to wash them.

As the boy prepared Hannah's coffee, he talked. He talked a lot, and quickly, jumping from subject to subject, his hands moving all the while. But Hannah was still on her guard. Too much had happened too quickly for her to trust anyone at this point.

The boy said he was an avid fan of American films. Did she watch American films? No? But they were the best! He said everything that needed to be known could be learned from American movies, which is why he had dropped out of school, and his name was Samir Yusef, but everyone called him George Clooney—just like the famous American actor—because Samir was so handsome and was always kissing the girls. He said he was also an excellent dancer and on the instant began clapping a complex rhythm above his head and sashaying his hips until his uncle, the proprietor of the coffee stand, smacked the back of his head.

The boy rubbed his scalp, scowling at his uncle.

"You are French?" he asked Hannah.

"I am from Brussels. From Belgium."

"Your accent sounds French," he said, pouring the coffee into a small white cup and passing it to her.

She took a sip. It was bitter. "We speak French in Belgium."

"French? Really?"

She nodded, taking another sip.

"Ah! Then I must help you," he declared.

She narrowed her eyes. "Why must you help me?"

"Because I am George Clooney! And you are a sad, pretty French girl, so lost in my city."

"I am not French, I am from—"

"And do you think I am handsome?"

Hannah assessed him, tapping her chin. "First, you are vain. You posture like a peacock, and your sunglasses are too big. But I confess you are handsome."

He grinned.

"Second! You look nothing like George Clooney. It is a ridiculous name. You must change it."

The boy looked aghast. He opened his mouth to protest.

"Third!" she interrupted. "If you are eighteen then I will eat my shoes. Right here on the spot."

He appeared more hurt than ever. "I am nearly eighteen. I do not look eighteen?"

"You are not a day older than eleven, and you know it. Now what is your guide fee? I must reach my grandfather at once."

He held up his hands in defence. "Easy! Take it easy! I will take you to your grandfather's home," he said. "In exchange for... a kiss."

She scowled with suspicion. "On the hand?"

"On the lips of course!"

She thought about this, tapping her chin.

"If you prove trustworthy, like a knight, and take me to my grandfather, then you will earn a kiss. That is fair. But not on the lips. It will be here."

She touched her left cheek.

"How close to the lips?" he asked.

They haggled for a while, until a distance of 1.5 inches from the lips was agreed upon for the placement of a kiss. But only after Clooney, which he insisted she call him, proved trustworthy and fulfilled his promise.

"Don't worry, I know all the shortcuts," Clooney assured her. He led her up the stone steps that climbed from the plaza. He had offered to help with her suitcase but she refused. Clunk, clunk, clunk went the suitcase. They emerged on a flat rooftop. Hannah saw couches and plastic chairs and a TV set balanced atop a milk crate and lots of laundry lines strung from aerial antennas. The rooftops of Jerusalem were where people relaxed in the cool of the evening. She and Clooney crossed the rooftop, descended down another set of steps, and suddenly Hannah found herself in someone's home.

"Is this your home?" she asked.

"No."

Spread upon cushions on the carpeted floor, a family ate dinner around a pot of rice and vegetables. Clooney said something in Arabic, they said something back, and with no further explanation, he directed Hannah through the kitchen, down a hall with old photos of mustachioed men on the walls, and finally into the washroom. He hopped onto the sink, opened the window and clambered out, dropping to the cobbles of yet another alley on the far side.

Hannah's head was spinning. "Whose home is this?" she called down from the window.

"Pass me your suitcase," he said, reaching up.

Reluctantly, she passed him her suitcase.

"Now you," he said, helping Hannah down into the alley.

Landing safely in the alley, she brushed the grit from her hands and smoothed her summer dress. "Thank you," she said. "That was quite interesting. I still have no—"

At the sound of Hannah's voice, four young men, who were lingering on the steps of a nearby shop, looked up. Clooney went rigid.

"Are they friends of yours?" she asked.

The four young men stood as one.

"This way," said Clooney, turning brusquely in the opposite direction and leading Hannah away.

"Do you know them?" Hannah repeated, checking her shoulder. All four of the young men were now following.

"Yes," he said. "This way." He yanked her down another alley and then down a flight of steps.

"Are we in trouble?" she asked.

Clooney said nothing. Then he paused, "What is in your suitcase?"

"My things."

"Do you need them?"

"Of course I need them!"

"Then we will come back for them. But we must escape."

"Escape?"

Clooney tugged the suitcase from her grip and wheeled it into the nearest shop and yelled orders at the shopkeeper, who quickly stowed it behind the counter.

"It is safe," he said.

"For you, perhaps. But I could never find this place again."

"Come, we must hurry!"

"I am not going anywhere until you tell me what is happening. Why are those boys after you?"

"An old matter. Nothing to do with you."

"What does that mean?"

He sighed. "I swindled them."

Hannah squared both fists upon her hips. "You assured me you were trustworthy!"

"For you, yes!"

"I do not see the difference."

"They are swindlers themselves," he said, as though nothing could be more obvious. "Swindling is all they understand. If I did not sometimes give them a proper swindling, how could they ever trust me?"

"Your logic is ridiculous. I expect you will now try to swindle me as well."

"Never! You are a pretty French girl, sad and alone, and I am your brave rescuer!"

"First, I do not need rescuing. Second, stop saying I am sad. Just because I wear a dress does not mean I dislike adventure. Third, I am not French. I am from Bel—"

Clooney grabbed her wrist and jerked Hannah into a run just as the thugs appeared in the alley.

Sprinting now, Clooney led Hannah into an open marketplace. Evening was upon the city, and the market stalls were festooned with long, looping chains of tiny colored lights. It was like a festival, with the smells and smoke of cooked meat hazing the multi-colored dimness. Clooney pulled her left, then right, dodging between vendors and then halted as the thugs unexpectedly cut them off.

"Now what?" asked Hannah, the two of them slowly backing up.

In a flash, Clooney whipped a slingshot from his back pocket, loaded it with a stone from the market floor, and fired. The stone knocked the leg from a table stacked with tomatoes. The tomatoes crashed to the floor, and the thugs slipped and stumbled into a pile of twisting arms and legs.

Before the boys regained their feet, Clooney led Hannah out of the marketplace and they sprinted up another set of steps to the nearest roof. Up top, there were laundry lines and TV antennas, potted plants, and a rusty old bike. But no exit. They were trapped.

Looking frantically about, Hannah saw a heap of peppers drying upon a plastic tarp. She had an idea.

"Help me fold the tarp," she said, and together she and Clooney wrapped the peppers within and then stomped them into a fine red dust. Hannah carried the bundled tarp to the edge of the roof. She peered over the edge. Just below, she saw the four thugs racing for the steps that led to her rooftop. She opened the tarp and heaved its contents into the air. The pepper dust rained down onto the boys, and they swatted at the burning cloud, rubbing their eyes, which only made it worse.

"Good thinking!" said Clooney.

Hannah smiled proudly.

In the alley below them, the thugs yelled and cursed and coughed and cried.

"No time to waste. Quickly, follow me," said Clooney, racing to the nearest TV antenna. A cable was strung from it, swooping over the cobbled alley thirty feet below, eventually tying off to another TV antenna on the far side.

"Can you make it?" Clooney asked, still uncertain what kind of girl he had along.

"Yes," Hannah replied, and she reached for the cable. But Clooney stopped her, insisting that he, as her brave hero, must cross the clothesline first to test its safety.

He grabbed hold of the cable. Hand over hand, he began working his way across. Just before reaching the far side, they both heard an ominous creak, and one of the antennas began to tilt. Clooney completed the last few moves and dropped safely on the far side.

"Quickly!" he yelled. "They are coming!"

Hannah looked up at the cable. She tested the pole of the antenna, giving it a shake. It wobbled in its footing.

At that moment, the four thugs topped the roof and skidded to a halt.

"Now!" yelled Clooney.

With no other choice, Hannah reached for the cable and started across. Midway, she paused and looked down. She saw the busy alley far below, people and carts going to and fro. In her hesitation, she heard another creak and felt the cable dip a few inches as the antenna's weakened pole began to lean.

"Hurry!" Clooney called. "The antenna is falling! Hurry!"

Hannah reached for the next handhold and suddenly the antenna leaned further. And then her gut clenched as the antenna tipped completely and crashed against the side of the roof, the cable dropping another ten feet.

Hannah swung precariously from the cable, struggling to keep her grip. Looking down, she saw a canvas awning slung from one wall of the alley.

"Swing!" Clooney yelled, instructing her to swing toward the awning and drop onto it. Hannah tried, but she couldn't. She could barely hold on. She knew, in that instant, she was going to fall.

Clooney backed up on the opposing roof. He got a running start and then leapt over the edge, wrapping both arms around Hannah as they collided midair. The impact of his weight swung them both toward the awning, and together they dropped onto the soft fabric, cushioning their fall, before sliding safely to the street below.

They faced each other, hands on their knees, panting with exhilaration.

"Just like in the movies!" declared Clooney.

"That was fantastic!" Hannah agreed, catching her breath.

"Was I brave?"

She smiled and nodded. "Very."

"Was I trustworthy?"

Hannah stifled a laugh. "Perhaps you are pushing it."

"Perhaps," he said, casually looking off to the left, which exposed his right cheek as he tapped it, "this is the part where the sad, lost French girl decides to kiss her brave hero…"

Four angry faces suddenly appeared on the rooftop above, the thugs yelling threats and shaking their fists in the air.

"Not yet it isn't," she said, and this time it was she who grabbed his wrist and yanked Clooney away as they escaped into the crowded labyrinth of old Jerusalem.

"Here we are," said Clooney as they entered the Jewish Quarter. "Just as I promised. Is any of this familiar?"

Hannah looked about. It was certainly the Jewish Quarter. She could tell in an instant because every single man was dressed identically in a black suit, black tie, black-brimmed hat, and forelocks. Forelocks were like long curls that were sometimes a foot or more long, hanging just in front of each ear.

She had once asked Henri why all the men dressed the same in the Jewish Quarter. And Henri had answered in his most scholarly voice, "I have no idea, my dear. None at all. I am Jewish myself, and it is still a mystery. But where would we be without our mysteries?"

After a brief laugh, he explained further. He said these men were called orthodox Jews. That meant they followed the Jewish religion according to its most ancient traditions and laws. The orthodox had dressed this way for hundreds of years, and for some people, Henri said, it was enough to do a thing because others had done it before. But most importantly, their unusual traditions added spice to Jerusalem, which Henri never opposed, and Hannah had since come to feel the same.

As Hannah glanced about, she thought she recognized a nearby café. She headed in that direction, and then a bakery became familiar too. She knew where she was.

"This way," she said. "We are close. Henri's home is just up here."

They climbed the road winding up a steep hill. The buildings on either side were slightly more modern. There were street lamps lighting the way. They came to Henri's door and Hannah paused, suddenly anxious.

This was it, Henri's home. She looked for a light in the upstairs window, but saw none. She realized she had placed all hope in reaching this place, as if some magical safety were guaranteed. But the reality was nothing had gone right today, and there was no reason to believe this would be different. And if Henri wasn't here, she really had no idea what to do next.

"Look!" said Clooney, pointing to the front door. The jam was cracked, and the door hung askew from its hinges. It had been forced open.

Hannah's pulse raced. Her worst fears were confirmed.

"Hannah, wait!" said Clooney. "Where are you going?"

"I am going in."

"I don't know, Hannah. Shouldn't we—"

Hannah shoved the broken door open and entered the apartment. Clooney hurried to catch up.

The foyer was small, simply a place to enter Henri's home and hang a coat or scarf on the rack by the staircase. It was very quiet. All appeared normal. Perhaps Hannah's imagination had run away with her, and Henri was upstairs, waiting for her in his cozy Venetian chair, reading beside the fire. Hoping beyond hope, she raced up the stairs to the apartment's main floor and halted with a gasp before the living room.

It was destroyed. Everything was overturned. The shelves were ripped down. The television was in pieces. The red velvet couch was slashed open, its stuffing yanked out. The blinds hung in tatters. Henri's chair, his special Venetian where he read, had been splintered like kindling before the fireplace.

Hannah was horrified. Without thinking, she called Henri's name, loudly, but no one responded. With her hand against her mouth, she knew, without even needing to search the other rooms, that Henri would not be inside this apartment.

The Cancellarii had kidnapped her grandfather.

But had they found the map? The treasure map Hannah was meant to protect?

No, she realized. They hadn't found it. That was why they took Henri away, and that was why they were following her. They must know Henri had given her secret instructions to find it.

Frantically, Hannah began sifting through the debris, searching for some clue. Some hint Henri might have left for her to follow. Her grandfather often contrived complex riddles for her to solve, complete with messages hidden about the apartment, or written in code, or Egyptian hieroglyphs (which he taught her to read) or even ancient Sumerian (which she was still learning).

She started down the hall.

"Where are you going now? What are you looking for?" asked Clooney.

Hannah stopped and looked at him. "Do you still wish to help me?"

"Yes."

"Can you keep a secret?"

He nodded.

"I am searching for a map. A treasure map."

Clooney's eyes went big. "What kind of treasure?"

"I don't know. A treasure. It does not matter. I just know it must be found, and my grandfather is in danger until I find the map."

They checked the bedroom. The mattress was flipped against the wall and slashed underneath, the sheets in a tangled ball. The closet had been ransacked, its boxes emptied and strewn about. She searched the den. Every book on every shelf had been tossed into a heap in the middle of the floor. The stereo was smashed. Pictures were torn from the wall. She picked one up, shaking the broken glass from the frame.

"Is that your grandfather?" asked Clooney.

Hannah nodded.

In the photograph, she and Henri were squatting side-by-side at a dig site in Jerusalem. Henri's white hair was blown across his eyes, his bushy white mustache arched in a grin. He was pointing out some detail in the layout of the foundation stones they were uncovering. Hannah was holding back her blonde hair with one hand, smiling as well. She remembered that day. It was only last year.

Hannah carefully placed the ruined photo atop the stereo. She returned to the kitchen. There she found the cabinet doors hung open, the dishes shattered on the floor. Nothing seemed to have escaped the demolition. She pressed her palms to her cheeks, looking about at the mess. Her skin prickled with fear. Her whole body was trembling.

She took three deep breaths, telling herself to calm down. To think. Next, she unzipped her backpack and took out the book. She opened the front cover and once again studied the note Henri had written.

1. Keep the map safe
2. Beware the *Cancellarii*
—

5. Remember, Hannah, you have the magic eye!

There was more to this message, she knew it. She started thinking about how Henri had removed numbers 3 and 4 from the list, not because they were hidden, but simply to draw her attention elsewhere. Was it possible the remaining numbers 1, 2, and 5, had meaning too? What might they lead to? Where would she even look? And what if...

She put the numbers together: 125

On impulse, she turned to page 125 of *An Illustrated Guidebook To Israel's Historic Sites*. And there it was. The answer she was looking for.

On a page describing the building materials used to make ancient homes, there was a picture of a stone hearth, or fireplace. And the picture was circled. Henri had circled it.

"The fireplace!" she said.

She and Clooney raced back to the living room. Going straight to the fireplace, Hannah reached up into the chimney and immediately felt a small nook cut into the stones. And there was something inside. She pulled it out and found herself holding a book in her hands. A very old book. The leather cover was battered and worn.

"Is this what you were looking for?" asked Clooney.

Hannah opened the cover. She looked at the first page. There was no doubt in her mind that Henri meant for her to find this. But if this was a map, thought Hannah, it was unlike any map she had ever seen before.

The book in Hannah's hands was clearly a journal. It was written long ago by someone named Julien Dubuisson. An ancestor perhaps? Julien's journal entries were all written in French. The first entry described a journey from France to Jerusalem and talked of sailing conditions, and the captain's demeanor, and the poor quality of food on the ship.

The second entry was entirely different. No longer a travel journal, it spoke of treasure. This journal, Julien said, could be used as a map to find the treasure.

Whereas most maps showed streets and avenues and highways, Julien's map consisted of seven hand-drawn illustrations. He had sketched them with pencil, and they were spread all throughout the journal. Each illustration was of an actual location in Israel, though exactly where in Israel, Hannah couldn't tell. Most unusual of all, Julien had drawn all seven illustrations *upside down*.

Clooney was at this point unable to contain himself. "What does it say, Hannah? Is this the map?"

"It is," she said. "But I still have no idea what it leads to. Look, you see these illustrations?"

Clooney nodded. "Why are they upside down?"

"I don't know. But they were drawn by someone named Julien Dubuisson, and they are like a code. Once you crack the code, these illustrations will lead you to the treasure."

They studied the first illustration together. Julien had drawn a large body of water, like a sea, with smoky mountains in the background.

"It's the Dead Sea," she said.

"How do you know?"

"Because it's written right here. And that's my grandfather's writing. His notes are everywhere."

All through the journal, Hannah recognized her grandfather's neat hand. He had packed his comments into the margins, between paragraphs, going sideways up the spine, just about anywhere he could find space to write. And right there, just beneath the illustration, Henri had written "the Dead Sea." The illustration was upside down, which was strange in itself. But most unusual of all, her grandfather had also written three numbers.

f.4   18   400

As an archaeologist, Henri loved anything to do with codes, hieroglyphs, ancient symbols.

"And what do you think those numbers mean?" asked Clooney.

She shut the journal, considering what this meant. "I think Henri cracked the code, and these numbers are the key," she said. "I think he solved the map. He knows where the treasure is hidden. And that's why the Cancellarii have finally made their move."

"But you have the map now," said Clooney, pointing worriedly at the journal. "Which means the people who took your grandfather… they will now be after you."

"They already are. Listen, I need more time here. There are more clues, and I must find them before the Cancellarii return. But I need you to get the police. They can help."

Clooney agreed. He sprinted off to fetch help, while Hannah gazed around at the wreckage of the apartment. When she said there were more clues here, she meant it. Clues were Henri's specialty.

She wandered slowly back through the house, going room to room, reexamining all she saw. This delicate glass sculpture that lay unbroken on its side—did that mean something? And over here, by the telephone, a notepad with scribbles—a secret message? A hint? Anything and everything was potentially a clue, but which ones really mattered? A detective would know the answer. So would an archaeologist.

Hannah hopped up onto the kitchen counter and just sat for a moment. She needed to slow down. So much was happening. A part of her wanted to pound her fists on the counter and scream like a child, and she was sincerely considering this option when she noticed a box on the floor. It was a pastry box. The box was pink with black writing on the lid, and it was half-buried beneath the skillets and broken dishes and utensils on the kitchen floor.

The thing was, Hannah already knew what was inside the box. It could only be one thing: Baklava. The honey-drizzled pastry she loved so much. It was unspoken tradition that Henri always had a box of Baklava waiting for Hannah when she arrived.

Hannah hopped back down from the counter and carefully dug the box out. She opened it. Among the gooey pastries, covered in shaved almonds and pistachios and sprinkles of chocolate, she saw the oddest thing.

Coiled like a serpent in the middle of the pastries was a belt. It was Henri's belt.

Why would Henri hide his belt in a box of pastries?

On closer inspection she noticed writing on the belt. It was written with a thick black marker, and hurriedly by the look of it, for none of the letters were straight. Looking closer still, Hannah realized no matter how hurriedly Henri had written those letters, haste couldn't explain why they rested at such odd angles.

Hannah wracked her memory, running through every cipher Henri had taught her, until she recalled one of the first codes she ever learned. When Henri had shown her, he had used a ribbon in his example, but a belt would work exactly the same. The code required that the ribbon be wrapped around a cylinder, like the leg of a table for instance, and then the message was written vertically upon the wrapping.

To make the letters on the belt line up, Hannah would need to find the same cylinder Henri had used to write the message. She tried the bannister of the stairs. After winding the belt three or four times around, she could already see it was wrong. None of the letters lined up.

Hannah dug out the leg of his Venetian chair from the wreckage by the fireplace. She wrapped the belt. Again, wrong. She tried the table. She tried the pole of the coat rack in the foyer. She tried the rod from the blinds which had been ripped down from the window. Nothing worked. The letters wouldn't line up. She tried every cylindrical item she could find in the house and then...

Henri's nightcane! That's what he called the cane he used for his special walks at night. Though her grandfather was fit from all his years of working outdoors, walking alone at night through the lightless alleys of the Old City of Jerusalem was not for the faint of heart, so Henri brought his cane as protection. The cane was heavy, made of pure ebony with a solid brass cap. A sturdy weapon if swung with force.

But the cane wasn't in its usual place by the door. Hannah rummaged all through the house, searching each room until she found the nightcane leaning against the wall in the den between the grandfather clock and the remains of the bookcase. She stood there in the small, protected hollow. She wrapped the belt around the cane, whispering to herself, "Please Henri, give me a clue. Who are the Cancellarii? Where were you taken?"

When she completed the last coil, the letters lined up perfectly:

Andrepont

A name. Andrepont was a name, a French name. But who was it?

Hannah looked down, studying both the belt and the cane, trying to make sense of it all. For the famous archaeologist, Henri Dubuisson, expert in ancient enigmas, symbols, hidden codes, everything had a meaning. Everything. If she knew Henri—and as his granddaughter, she did—it was no mistake Hannah was now standing here, in the most concealed part of his home, with two things in her hand:

1. A weapon
2. A name

She had no doubt one was now meant for the other.

Hannah heard a noise on the stairwell. She froze, straining to hear if—there! She heard it again! Someone was climbing the stairs. Hannah crouched behind the grandfather clock with cane in hand. Could it be Clooney? No, she heard voices. Several voices. The Cancellarii then? Had they returned to search for the journal once more? Or perhaps they had seen Hannah entering the apartment and were now coming for her!

Whomever it was had just entered the living room. There were many of them, and their muffled voices reached Hannah as they roved freely about house, flipping through debris. Now she heard voices in the hall, just beyond the den. Men's voices, speaking loudly, and coming closer...

"Looks like the den is down here," someone was saying, "and look at all those books!"

Tightening her grip on the cane, Hannah leapt out from her hiding place, prepared to brain the nearest intruder, and then let the cane drop in relief.

It was the police. Clooney had fetched the police, just like she'd asked, and now three officers stood before her, looking as startled as she felt.

"Who are you?" they asked, clearly not expecting to find a fierce, cane-wielding Belgian child hiding amongst the ruins of a crime scene.

"I am Hannah Dubuisson, granddaughter of Henri Dubuisson, who has been kidnapped by the Cancellarii, a very old and dangerous secret society of treasure hunters who will stop at nothing to steal their prize! You must find them at once!"

The officers shared a look. One of them placed a hand on Hannah's shoulder. "Perhaps we should start at the beginning," he said.

While the officer took Hannah aside for questioning, the housed filled up with Israeli police.

Everywhere Hannah looked, uniformed officers snooped about, snapping photos of the destruction that was once Henri's home.

"And you say a secret organization of treasure hunters called the…" the officer checked his notes, "…called the *Cancellarii*, did all this?"

Hannah nodded.

The officer shut his notebook and gave her a dubious look. "I don't know how to tell you this Ms. Dubuisson. Jerusalem has a lot people who don't get along. A lot of problems. But kidnappings by ancient secret societies just isn't one of them. Did your grandfather ever discuss any enemies? Anyone who might have wanted to do him harm?"

"Yes!" Hannah shouted with exasperation. "I already told you! He warned me to look out for—"

"Ah! The inspector is here," the officer interrupted. "Perhaps he can sort this out."

Hannah turned to see a tall, broad-shouldered man enter the living room and glance about at the mess. He wore a grey linen suit with a black turtleneck. He had piercing dark eyes that took in the apartment at a glance, assessed it, and concluded it was bad, very bad. The inspector was clearly not a happy man.

Hannah's officer raised a hand, waving the inspector over. "Inspector Andrepont!" he called. "Over here sir. Perhaps you can help. This young lady is the granddaughter of the missing man and has some interesting ideas about the culprit."

Andrepont! The inspector was the man Henri had warned her about! But then, Hannah reminded herself, Henri had also taught her not to jump to conclusions. She knew nothing about this Andrepont. Perhaps he had nothing to do with the Cancellarii.

Inspector Andrepont moved with calm authority, his gaze locked on Hannah as he crossed the room.

"Mademoiselle Dubuisson, how do you do?" he said in flawless French. How did he know Hannah spoke French?

Don't jump to conclusions… Don't jump to conclusions…

"This must be distressing," he said. "To discover your grandfather is missing and find his home in disarray. You have my sympathy. However, it is very important I ask you some questions, as I am sure you understand. May I proceed?"

Hannah nodded, her gut clenching into a knot.

"If you do not mind," Inspector Andrepont said to the other officer. "I would like to speak with the Mademoiselle alone."

He gave Hannah a meaningful glance, and once the officer departed, the inspector simply looked at her. She waited for him to speak. After some moments he leaned forward, nearly hissing in her ear, "I know all about you. Your grandfather too."

Hannah froze, her breath caught in her throat.

The inspector continued, "I believe you have something of your grandfather's. Something of great importance," he whispered. "There are dangerous people about. More dangerous than you can imagine. Perhaps the item in your care would be safer with me."

It was a barely veiled threat, and Hannah was now trembling head to toe. There could now be no doubt: Andrepont was Cancellarii, and he wanted the map. She needed a way out.

Inspector Andrepont was about to speak again when the photo team entered and began snapping pictures of the crime scene. Andrepont acted as though nothing were unusual. "As I was saying," he said to Hannah. "We will do our utmost to find whoever kidnapped your grandfather. Our best detectives have already—"

"I must pee," she said.

Andrepont gave her a curious look. "Your pardon?"

"I must use the washroom."

The inspector frowned. "I see. Of course. Nature calls, as they say. But please return at once, as we still have much to discuss."

Hannah nodded and made a beeline across the living room, heading straight for the stairs, which would take her outside.

"Uh… Mademoiselle Dubuisson?" the inspector called.

Reluctantly, Hannah turned around.

"I believe the nearest washroom is over here. Is it not?" He pointed down the hall toward the bedroom.

"Yes, of course," she said. She smiled, doing her best to disguise her disappointment as she retraced her steps and headed down the hall. Once inside the washroom, she immediately locked the door behind her and heaved a deep breath to calm herself.

Now what? How would she ever sneak past the inspector to reach the stairs?

Someone knocked on the door. "Mademoiselle?" came the inspector's voice.

"A moment please!" she called. Without a second to lose, she flushed the toilet and turned on the faucet, using the noise of each to hide the squeaking of the window as she slid it open.

She peeked outside. It was a long drop. And no canopy to catch her this time.

Craning her head, she looked up, toward the roof. It was only a couple feet overhead. She saw no other choice. Biting her lip, she hauled herself out the window, balanced herself upon the sill, and reached up for the roof. A moment later she was standing safely atop her grandfather's building, her red backpack with the journal cinched tightly to her shoulders, and the whole of the Old City spreading below her. In the light of the rising moon, the countless domes and spires of the city's ancient temples left her spellbound, and she half expected Aladdin to arrive on his magic carpet and carry her away.

But this was not a fairytale, she quickly reminded herself. Henri was kidnapped, and Hannah was now on the run from both the Cancellarii *and* the Israeli police. And she didn't even have her suitcase! That scoundrel Clooney had probably sold half its contents by now, figuring she would never be able to locate it again.

Glowing with fury, and no small mixture of fear, Hannah hurried across the roof to the opposite side where the limbs of a great walnut tree brushed the building's side. Hannah worked her way onto the nearest limb, eventually shimmying her way down the trunk.

With both feet on the ground, she brushed her palms and turned around to find Clooney standing there, as though they had agreed to meet at this very spot.

"You!" she said, jabbing her finger into his chest. "What are you still doing here?"

"I did not get my kiss."

"For good reason! You swindler! How much did you earn for the sale of my suitcase?"

Clooney appeared hurt. He looked at her. "I knew you wouldn't be able to find it on your own. I waited here for you, so we could find it together."

Hannah stopped. She took a deep breath, recognizing the sincerity in his eyes. The truth was, Clooney was the only person who had done her a speck of kindness, and she was being unfair.

"You are right," she said. "I am sorry. Will you forgive me?"

Clooney's face lit up. "Done! Am I still your brave rescuer?"

A voice called down from the window above. "Mademoiselle Dubuisson? Is that you?"

Hannah and Clooney both looked up to find Inspector Andrepont leaning out the window. Hannah gulped. There was a moment of silence as they sized up the situation, and then the inspector held something before him, pointing it at her—a gun?

There was a flash of light, and Hannah was momentarily blinded. When her vision cleared she saw the inspector holding a phone. He had just taken a photo of both Clooney and herself.

Clooney took her hand, and they sprinted into the night.

After retrieving Hannah's suitcase as promised, Clooney led her back to the rooftop above his uncle's coffee stall. He brought her a blanket and a pillow. He assured her, "No one comes up here. You will be safe."

"But what if the police come looking?"

Clooney chuckled. "We are Palestinians. No one here tells the Israeli police anything."

"I mean you," she said. "They have your picture too. I am afraid we are now in this together."

Clooney shrugged, unconcerned. But the reality was, the Israeli police—one of whom was clearly a member of the Cancellarii—now had their photos, which would likely be broadcast across the whole of Israel. Come morning, both forces would be searching for Hannah and Clooney.

Clooney's uncle called from below.

"I must go. I would invite you in, but..."

Hannah nodded. "I understand. I am a Jewish girl, and you are a Palestinian boy, and your family might object. Clooney, don't worry. I will be comfortable here."

His uncle called again, and Clooney waved before departing.

Hannah lay upon her back, looking up at the stars, the sounds of the city all around. She tried to piece together everything that had happened today, and what she must do tomorrow. She came up with a list of five questions she should answer if she was to solve this mystery and find her grandfather.

1. What does the map lead to?
2. Why are the illustrations drawn upside down?
3. Why did Henri write three numbers beneath each illustration?
4. What is the magic eye?
5. Who was Julien Dubuisson?

She realized the last question should be the first, as it all started with Julien, and the answer was likely no farther away than her backpack.

She sat up and removed the journal. By moonlight, she opened the leather cover and chose a page at random. She began reading and was immediately enthralled. According to Henri's notes, Julien Dubuisson was Hannah's great-great-great-great-great-great-great-grandfather, and was a true Renaissance man in the court of Emperor Napoleon Bonaparte and about the most interesting person Hannah had ever heard of. Julien spoke eleven languages. He was an accomplished painter, sculptor, and violinist. He was a mathematician and a scholar of the kabbalah, which was the most mystical of the Jewish texts. He was also a documented explorer and, according to this journal, a powerful *sorcier*, or sorcerer, with unusual talents—making him the prize of Napoleon's court.

It was around the year 1790 that Julien Dubuisson first approached Emperor Napoleon and requested permission and funds to hunt for a lost treasure in Jerusalem. A treasure so vast, he said, that it boggled the mind. Once Julien recovered this treasure, he promised to return it to Napoleon for the glory of France.

Emperor Napoleon was one of the few rulers who openly supported the Jews of Europe at that time. As a token of the confidence and respect he held for his sorcerer, Napoleon gave Julien Dubuisson the blessing of France, a large bag of coins, and sent him on his way.

But Julien Dubuisson never returned to France. Nor did he ever send gold or jewels or any evidence of the famed treasure. The only thing he sent back to France was a solitary journal, which he insisted was a 'map'.

Crafty magician that he was, Julien Dubuisson did not give specific instructions to find the treasure. He instead created seven enchanted illustrations, each one encoded with clues to the next. The map, and the enchanted illustrations it was made of, could only be deciphered with a "magic eye."

Hannah stopped reading.

There it was again: The magic eye. Hannah sensed the magic eye somehow tied it all together. Perhaps Henri had one and had used it to crack the code. Maybe it even explained the three numbers he had written.

A plan was forming in Hannah's mind. The Cancellarii had Henri and wanted the map she now held. She in turn wanted Henri and would do anything to get him back. Perhaps they could arrange an exchange. The treasure map for her grandfather. But of course, on further thought, she realized the Cancellarii would never give Henri up. The map was useless without him, for Henri Dubuisson alone could read it.

Which left only one option.

To find the treasure herself. With the treasure in hand, Hannah could certainly ransom it back for her grandfather.

How exactly she would decipher the map's code, locate the treasure, and trade it for Henri's freedom, she didn't yet know. But it was late, and Hannah was more exhausted than she could ever recall. She told herself to let it go for now. To sleep on it.

She lay back down. She clicked on her cellphone, gazing at the home screen.

"Just let it go," she whispered aloud. "Just let it go…"

Unfortunately, for Hannah Dubuisson, letting things go had never come easy.

⬯

Hannah woke to find the sun shining in her eyes, and Clooney squatting beside her and smiling in his blue T-shirt and giant sunglasses. In his left hand was a small silver pot of coffee and in his right hand a white cup. She sat up, looking about the rooftop, the view of Jerusalem all around her.

"Sleep well?" he asked, deftly pouring coffee into the cup.

She shook her head, accepting the coffee. She breathed in the aroma of cardamom and took a sip. "I have an idea though."

"Will it get your grandfather back?"

"Perhaps. If my plan works. My grandfather has a friend at the university. Her name is Professor Weisman. She has known me all my life and may have information about this journal. She might be able to help."

Hannah finished the coffee in a single gulp and returned the cup. "Oh yes, I almost forgot. Also, we are going on a treasure hunt."

Clooney smacked his hands together. "Fantastic! When do we start?"

"Right away." Hannah clicked on her cellphone.

Clooney peeked over her shoulder. "Who is that?" he asked, noting the picture of Hannah with her father.

"Me," she said, dialing Professor Weisman's number from her contact list.

"But you are so young in that photo. Why don't you change it?"

"Do you see that man? The man I am sitting with?"

"Yes."

"He is my father."

"Why is he not here in Jerusalem?"

"Hang on. Hello? Professor Weisman? This is Hannah Dubuisson. Yes, Henri's granddaughter. In Jerusalem, yes. Actually, I wonder if I could meet with you this morning. There is something I need to discuss. Oh, thank you, that is very kind. Yes, I will take a bus. I will be right over."

Hannah hung up and returned the phone to her backpack.

"Because he is dead," she said to Clooney.

The university was not in the Old City of Jerusalem, but in the new Jerusalem with its glass-windowed skyscrapers and boutiques and taxis honking horns. Coming from the Muslim Quarter of the Old City, it was like being catapulted a thousand years into the future.

Clooney and Hannah purchased two bus tickets, and along the way to the university she explained everything she knew about Julien Dubuisson, his mysterious journal, and the Cancellarii who were now after the both of them. She also described her plan to find the treasure and exchange it for Henri's freedom.

"This is perfect!" said Clooney. "Just like the movies!"

"It is not a movie," she assured him. "This is real. And if we make mistakes, people might get hurt. Try to be serious."

Hannah and Clooney hopped out at the university bus stop. They crossed the wide lawn and entered the huge building devoted entirely to archaeology. They went straight up to Professor Weisman's office on the fifth floor.

"So good to see you Hannah! My, how you have grown!"

Professor Weisman was an older woman, gracious and polite, with short grey hair, bright blue eyes, and a rather strong chin. Her office looked like the entire archaeological wing of a museum had been crammed into a single room. The desk was completely lost beneath boxes with mysterious labels and maps of ongoing digs. Various artifacts, statuary, and primitive stone tools filled the shelves and every available space on the floor. The bookshelves were packed, and even the wall was crowded with Professor Weisman's many certificates and awards in archaeology.

Hannah loved Weisman's office. She would have liked nothing more than to spend the rest of the day exploring the bookshelves and boxes with their treasure-trove of artifacts. Once, Weisman had invited Hannah to help her for an afternoon, and they spent three hours sitting cross-legged on the floor, recording and labeling rusty coins from a shoebox the professor had filled at a dig site near Bethlehem.

Professor Weisman poured tea and invited Hannah and Clooney to sit. "So what brings you here, Hannah? Everything going well?"

Where to start? Best to get straight to the point. "Henri has been kidnapped."

Professor Weisman was shocked and dismayed, and Hannah explained how Henri's home had been ransacked by the Cancellarii.

"The Cancellarii, really?" Professor Weisman seemed surprised. "Why would you think the Cancellarii are involved?"

"Because Henri told me so."

"Oh?"

"In a journal. I found a special journal."

Professor Weisman leaned forward. "You say Henri gave you a journal?"

Hannah nodded. "I was hoping you could tell me about the Cancellarii. I can't find any information online."

"And you won't," replied Weisman. "Few people have even heard of it."

"But you have. What do you know?"

"No more than what Henri has shared, from one colleague to another. I am no expert, but your family appears to be quite deeply connected to the court of Napoleon Bonaparte. So too are the Cancellarii. You see, when your great ancestor, Julien Dubuisson, left France to hunt for the lost treasure of King Solomon's temple—"

"King Solomon's temple?" Hannah interrupted. The lost treasure of King Solomon's temple was one of Henri's favorite topics. He raved about it.

"Well, of course," replied Weisman. "King Solomon's treasure is what Napoleon sent Julien to find."

If this was true, Hannah knew this wasn't just any treasure. "Solomon's temple was supposedly *covered* in gold. Every inch of it. And silver too."

"How much is it worth?" asked Clooney. "A million dollars?"

Professor Weisman considered the question. "The price of gold is always changing. Still, I've heard estimates placing the treasure at… oh… somewhere around fifty-six billion dollars."

Clooney's jaw dropped. "Did you say billion?"

"Dollars, yes. Fifty-six billion, or so I've heard. It's the largest unrecovered treasure in the history of the world."

Hannah felt a pit in her belly. Fifty-six. *Billion*. Dollars. No wonder the Cancellarii were so eager to find it. For that much gold, greedy men would do anything. Hurt anyone. Suddenly Hannah had a new and dreadful appreciation for the stakes.

Professor Weisman continued, "When Julien Dubuisson failed to return to France and furthermore failed to send treasure, there were some among Napoleon's court who believed France had been cheated."

"Cheated? But he sent a map!" argued Hannah, feeling protective of her family name.

"True. But a map no one could read. Except of course for our dear Henri, if what he told me is accurate. Nevertheless, some of Napoleon's court felt France was entitled to Solomon's treasure so long as they possessed the map. They formed a group, a small society of members with one purpose in mind: the recovery of King Solomon's treasure. This society took their name from the chancellors of justice in ancient Rome, calling themselves the Cancellarii. And they have spent the last two hundred years chasing clues in search of their treasure."

"So there are two maps then," said Hannah. "The Cancellarii's and then Henri's."

"A copy was made, yes. One copy stayed within the Dubuisson family when they fled to Belgium. The other remained with the Cancellarii. But unfortunately for the Cancellarii, their map remains encoded, while only Henri knows the secret to deciphering it."

"That would explain the kidnapping," said Hannah. "When the Cancellarii could not find Henri's map in his apartment, they took Henri instead, so he could decipher their own map."

"You are a sharp girl," said Weisman. "Sharp as ever. I trust you understand the danger this puts you in?"

Hannah nodded.

"One more thing," added Weisman. "This Inspector. This Andrepont you spoke of. I fear your suspicions are correct. Stay clear of Andrepont at all costs. He may even be their Grand Chancellor."

"Grand Chancellor?"

"The present leader of the Cancellarii. His position within the Israeli police force would only add to their power. Their ability to gather and track information will be immense."

Hannah took a deep breath. She knew what she had to do, and there was no time to waste.

"Thank you Professor Weisman. I must go now."

"Go? But where to, Hannah? You are too young to be alone."

"I am not alone. I have my friend, George Clooney."

Weisman gave Clooney a doubtful look. "Listen, I have a better idea. There is room for both of you in my home. Stay with me until this mess is resolved. Perhaps we can even look at this journal together and see if there is something we can do."

"But Professor Weisman," said Hannah. "There is no time to lose. Every moment I am safe in your home is a moment I could be searching for Henri."

"I insist, dear. And that is final. Henri would want it this way. Besides—"

At that moment, Professor Weisman's phone rang. She picked up the receiver but did not speak at once, staring back and forth between Hannah and Clooney. She listened for all of ten seconds and then said, "Right now? I'm in the middle of something *very important*. What? Why can't Jurowitz take care of it? Oh, for heaven's sake, I will be right there."

She hung up, looking distinctly frazzled.

"I apologize," said Weisman, attempting to compose herself. "There is a matter I must attend to. Make yourselves comfortable and I will be back shortly. Then we can get the two of you properly settled in."

Professor Weisman hurried from the office. A moment after shutting the door, Hannah heard the distinct sound of a key locking the door from the outside.

Hannah rushed for the door. "She locked us in!" she yelled.

"Your professor friend is very serious about keeping you safe."

"What about the window?"

"Too high," said Clooney. "We're five stories up."

Upon hearing this, Hannah herself looked up and found herself gazing at the drop-ceiling. Like most offices, the ceiling wasn't solid, but instead made of several light-weight interlocking tiles, all resting in an aluminum frame.

"The desk!" said Hannah, getting behind it and pushing. "Help me push the desk against the door."

"But why? Aren't we trying to get out?"

"Just help me."

Together they pushed the desk against the door and then Hannah climbed atop it. She reached up for the ceiling, and though she was closer, she still could not reach it. "Give me a hand," she said.

Clooney locked his fingers together and hefted Hannah up. She pushed against the ceiling tile and tossed it aside, peeking her head into the space above. It was dark, but she could see that the office wall did not extend higher than the drop ceiling. She could squirm through the ceiling space and over the wall, dropping into the hall on the far side.

"I found a way out," she said, "Just follow me." Together they crawled up and over. Removing yet another tile, they descended into the hall and were now free of the office and racing for the elevator.

On the ride down, Clooney said, "The professor seems to really care about you. Won't she be worried that you have disappeared?"

"That can't be helped," said Hannah. "We have a treasure to find, and the clock is ticking. There is one problem though."

"What is that?"

"The first point on the map. It's not in Jerusalem. It's at the Dead Sea."

"You still have money?" asked Clooney.

"Some, yes."

"Then leave it to me," said Clooney. "I'll get us on a bus."

As they exited the front doors of the university, Hannah noticed a security guard whisper into his radio. When they reached the lawn, she checked her shoulder and saw the guard watching her and Clooney.

"Did you notice that security guard?" asked Hannah once they reached the street and were out of sight.

"I did," said Clooney, stepping directly into traffic. Both lanes of cars screeched to a halt and honked their horns as Clooney led Hannah across the street. "And I did not like it. Come, let's hurry. The bus station is nearby."

The station was busy. Buses idled beside the curb, waiting for departure. As Hannah and Clooney walked along the pavement, looking for the correct bus, Hannah noticed the young Palestinian man on the motorcycle, the same one she had seen at the airport. He slowly patrolled the parking lot, looking left and right. How could the Cancellarii have been tipped off so quickly?

Without a moment to lose, Hannah shoved Clooney through the open doors of the nearest bus. Before he could even ask why, the doors shut with a bang and the bus lurched forward and departed the station.

"That was him," she breathed. "The man on the motorcycle I told you about."

Clooney peeked out the window and saw the man ride past the bus, still searching for Hannah.

"Where is this bus going?" he asked the driver.

"Masada," replied the driver.

"We're in luck," said Clooney. "The Dead Sea is on the way."

They purchased their tickets and took their seats near the back of the bus. She plugged her phone into the socket near the floor. The bus was crowded with tourists from every part of the world, with a few Palestinians mixed in. They were all headed to the ancient ruins of Masada, a popular destination for visitors.

But Hannah and Clooney would be jumping off early. The Dead Sea was only an hour from Jerusalem. Henri had once taken her there, and she thought it was perhaps the most unusual place she had ever been. The desert surrounding the Dead Sea was the lowest point of dry land on earth. The landscape was bleak and moonlike. And the seawater was so dense with salt, it was nearly impossible for swimmers to sink. Tourists read newspapers as they floated on their backs, bobbing atop the water as though upon inflatable rafts.

Fifteen minutes into their bus ride, they were already entering the desert. The landscape looked peeled, like someone had rolled back the earth's crust, revealing a raw, red-dish skin beneath. No trees grew and very few bushes. Rugged hills and even mountains rose in the distance.

Hannah said, "Will your parents be worried about you? Or wonder where you are?"

Clooney waved the thought away. "I live with my uncle. All he cares about is his coffee stall and making money. Money, money, money. As long as I don't create trouble, he does not care if I come or go."

Hannah wondered about Clooney's parents and where they were. Was his father gone, like hers? She waited for Clooney to say more, but he didn't, and though she wanted to ask about a thousand questions, she bit her lip and inquired no more.

They passed a road sign for 'Masada, 62 km.' Then another sign for 'The Pillar of Salt, 47 km.' Hannah was just beginning to settle into the ride, watching the desert fly by as she gazed out the window, when she heard the grinding of gears. The bus began to slow. Startled, she sat upright to peek through the front window and saw a military checkpoint up ahead. Israeli soldiers with machine guns had set up a blockade to inspect passing vehicles.

"Oh no," said Clooney. "This is not good."

Hannah had encountered many such checkpoints throughout her travels in the past. It was a hair-raising experi-ence for anyone to be questioned and sometimes frisked by soldiers with machine guns. The first time, she had felt fright-ened and confused, and she had many questions for Henri.

She remembers how Henri had smiled, placing his hand atop hers as he explained.

"My dear Hannah," he said. "Throughout history our people have been hurt many times. So we built a country strong enough to keep us safe, to stop others from hurting us again. Some people say these checkpoints protect our people. Others say they do more harm than good. The important thing, my dear, is to face them with the intrepid spirit of the explorer. You are an archaeologist! There is no room for fear in our profession."

So Hannah had grown accustomed to the long delays. She would generally keep her nose buried in a book, paying little attention as the guards searched through one car after another. But today was different. Were the soldiers in league with the police and therefore carrying a photograph of her and Clooney? It was impossible to say where the Cancellarii's power began and ended. As they approached the blockade, Hannah's pulse pounded in her ears.

She turned to Clooney, and he was white with fright. "Ideas?" he said.

"We go out the window," she said.

"The window? Are you crazy?"

"No. I don't know. Maybe. But we have to, we have no choice."

Hannah clicked the latches on the window and opened it. A blast of hot wind poured in, ruffling her hair. The bus was nearly at the checkpoint. She stuffed her phone into her backpack and shoved her backpack out the window. She climbed out after and dropped to the ground as the bus rolled to a halt. Clooney's feet slapped the asphalt beside her, and she snatched up the backpack and dashed for the bushes beside the road.

"Do you think anyone saw us?" she asked.

"Just every single person on the bus," said Clooney.

"Right. At least the soldiers with machine guns were too busy to—"

"Hey!" called one of the soldiers, pointing in their direction.

"Run!" yelled Clooney, and the children darted away, half-sprinting, half-tumbling into a low gulch beside the road. They scampered to another set of bushes, further from the checkpoint, and from there slunk down beside a large boulder, catching their breath as they hid from view.

"Do you think they can see us?" whispered Hannah.

Clooney brought a finger to his lips.

They could hear soldiers swatting through bushes above. They could hear the crackle of the soldiers' radios. One was speaking now.

"What are they saying?" asked Clooney.

Hannah's face went white. "They say they're coming down the gulch. They're coming right for us!"

Clooney removed his slingshot, showing it to Hannah.

"No!" she hissed. "They have guns!"

He shook his head, pointing silently to another set of bushes, roughly fifty meters away. Clooney loaded his slingshot with a stone and fired it at the bushes. It landed with a loud clunk among the rocks, and the soldiers glanced that way and then took up a run in that direction.

"It worked!" said Hannah. "They're leaving!"

Clooney grabbed Hannah's wrist and they hurried away, crouching low to stay hidden as they crept from bush to bush in the opposite direction of the soldiers. Ten minutes later they were alone in the desert, walking the base of an enormous red bluff. No road and no soldiers in sight. They may as well have been the only people on earth for the desolation of the place.

They paused for a breather in the shade of the bluff and Hannah unzipped her backpack. She handed Clooney a can of coke and a slightly crushed packet of airplane pretzels.

As they shared the snack, Clooney said, "The desert goes for miles. We'll never find the Dead Sea."

Hannah removed a compass from her backpack.

"You have a compass?" said Clooney with amazement.

"Of course," said Hannah, digging out her illustrated book on historic sites and opening it to a two-page spread showing a detailed map.

"This way," she said, pointing directly into the desert. She slipped the compass into the front pocket of her dress.

"And an umbrella?" said Clooney as she pulled it from her pack. She clicked a button on the handle and a bright red dome popped open above her head.

"You will thank me," she assured him. "Henri always says an umbrella is an archaeologist's second most important tool."

But Clooney refused to take shade beneath the umbrella, insisting it was un-heroic for a hero to accept such help from a sad French girl in distress.

"I am not French. I am from Belgium. I am not distressed because I have come prepared for the wilderness, whereas you are better suited for the dancehall. And I am not sad. In fact I am looking forward to our adventure."

Three hours later, they sat exhausted in the shade of a lone acacia tree. Since leaving the road, it was the first and only tree they had seen. They had finished their second can of coke and were still thirsty. Hannah's skin felt hot to the touch, and if her compass readings were correct, they were still several miles from the sea.

They finished off the pretzels, and Hannah handed Clooney a packet of handwipes.

He looked at the handwipes. "What don't you have in your backpack?"

She smiled. "Henri always taught me to be prepared. A good archaeologist never knows where the next great find is hiding and what you will need to find it."

"What else do you have in there?"

She began rummaging within the pack. "Not much. A book. Plus the journal. Let's see, a bit of rope. A pocketknife. Some money of course. My passport. Some pens. And my camera."

"You have a camera! You must take a picture of me!"

Clooney stood immediately and struck a pose against the trunk of the acacia, sliding his sunglasses low on the bridge of his nose. He looked ridiculous. Hannah snapped the photo, just to make him happy, and showed it to him.

He gazed at the image, his eyes clouded with longing. "I should not be here in the desert. I should be in Hollywood making films. Look at that face. Have you ever seen such a face?"

But Hannah was now distracted by something moving in the distance. She pointed into the desert. "Do you see that?" she asked. Far away, three black shapes wobbled in the heat waves. As the three shapes drew nearer, they became recognizable.

"I think they are camels," said Clooney.

The camels plodded slowly but steadily toward them, heading directly for the acacia tree just as Hannah and Clooney had, the only shaded cover for miles.

Soon Hannah could hear the bells that jangled from the camels' bridles, and she saw the Bedouin drivers riding atop them. Men of the desert, their eyes dark and unreadable. They parked their camels in a line before the children. Staring at them without a word from atop the twin humps of their beasts.

Each of the three men carried an umbrella.

The Bedouins were the nomads of this land, and they knew every ridge, every canyon, every shade-bearing tree and outcrop in this desert like the back of their hand. Hannah and Clooney were each hoisted atop a camel with little discussion. They glanced at each other, sharing a smile as they set out across the desert with their new friends leading the way.

The Bedouins didn't speak much, but they shared water and cashews, and by late afternoon, the hazy reflection of the

Dead Sea shone whitely in the distance. Hannah heard cars on the unseen highway that hugged the eastern shore.

The sun was setting when they reached the Dead Sea. The shore was white as snow, a beach made entirely of salt crystals. On the far side of the sea, the smoky mountains of Jordan shouldered into the darkening sky.

The Bedouins moved single file along the shore. Hannah had her journal out now, and she kept glancing down at the first illustration and then back to the sea in an attempt to match the exact location it was drawn from. She looked back and forth. Out on the water, she saw little islands of white crust, and places where the salt had gathered into strange alien mounds.

Soon the highway came into view, with cars and buses zipping along the two-lane road. Faces pressed against windows to glimpse the wondrous vision of two children riding camels along the white crystal shore of the Dead Sea, their Bedouin companions holding umbrellas against the pinking light of the sun.

As they traveled the shore, the sounds of a radio playing pop music drifted toward them. Then laughter and voices, and they soon came upon an encampment of tents perched beside the sea. People frolicked on the white beach, digging holes in the salt, tossing Frisbees, reading books, juggling soccer balls, and floating on the buoyant water.

"Hippies," said Clooney. "Americans."

"How can you tell?" asked Hannah.

He pointed to a cluster of bicycles, both large and small. Apparently they had all ridden here. "American hippies tour

Israel on bicycle this time of year. I don't know why, but it is common. You see them riding here. Though not usually with so many children."

Hannah noticed one man in particular. He was tall and skinny, with a thick beard and long dreadlocks down to his hip. He sat on the shore playing a flute. The sight was oddly beautiful.

Momentarily distracted by the little village and its unexpected activity, she almost forgot to check her journal. She glanced down, and realized the illustration lined up perfectly with her present view of the sea. It was an exact match.

"Stop," she told the camel driver. "We will get off here."

She and Clooney waved their thanks to the departing Bedouins and their camels and then returned their attention to the journal. Hannah flipped the illustration upside down for a better look. "This is the place," she said.

"It looks the same to me," Clooney agreed. "Those mountains in the background look exactly right. And that bend in the shore... I think your Julien was standing right here when he drew it. But why did he draw it upside down?"

It really was one of the strangest parts of this puzzle. Hannah could think of no good reason why Julien Dubuisson, a talented artist, would sketch his locations upside down. But the light was failing, and they would soon be in the dark. Hannah decided to snap a photo so she could study it later.

As she took off her backpack and began digging out her camera, something occurred to her. Her hand froze on the camera's pebbled grip.

"Are you all right?" asked Clooney. "You look like a statue."

"I just had a thought." She removed the camera. She gazed at it, tapping her chin. She looked at Clooney.

"I think I got it."

"Got what?" said Clooney with surprise.

"Henri is the one who taught me how to use a camera. Which, of course, he could not do without a history lesson. Did you know photography first began in this part of the world?"

Clooney shook his head.

"Look," she said, removing her phone. She saved all kinds of files on her phone, anything that might come in handy when you least expect it. She opened a file called "Camera Stuff" and scrolled through until she came to an entry about the history of cameras. "It says here, the first mention of a camera dates back to 1021. It was described by an Iraqi scientist in the Book of Optics. It wasn't until 1604 that the famous German astronomer, Johannes Keppler, named the device. He called it the *camera obscura*."

The website included a picture of the camera obscura. It was nothing like today's cameras. The device was basically a box with a pinhole on one side. "As the light of an image refracted through the pinhole," she read aloud, "it naturally projected itself upon the opposite wall of the camera—*upside down*."

"Upside down?" repeated Clooney. "So you think Julien Dubuisson used a camera obscura to sketch these pictures?"

"Of course!" said Hannah. "It all makes sense now. Henri told me about the Dutch painters who would place a thin piece of paper onto the projected image and then trace its detail. Even Leonardo Da Vinci wrote about it. The camera obscura was once a sensation in the art world."

Then Hannah gasped in her excitement, realizing there was more. "And if you were an artist at that time and suddenly you could draw what you saw with perfect detail... do you see what this means?"

"Not really," said Clooney.

She pointed to the image of the camera obscura on her phone, to the pinhole where the light passed through.

"For those artists, the pinhole of the camera obscura truly was a 'magic eye.' It allowed them to see and do what could not be done before."

Bingo. It all tied together. The mystery of the 'magic eye' and the upside down images came down to the same thing: Julien Dubuisson used a camera obscura to draw them.

Clooney looked at her. "Do you have a camera obscura?"

"No, but I have this." She held up the camera. "When Henri said I have the 'magic eye,' I think that was his clue. He was telling me I had everything I needed to decipher the map. It would have been too risky to write a full explanation on paper, so he did what he always does. He gave me a riddle."

"Let's see if you are right."

Her belly tingling with excitement, Hannah looked through the viewfinder of her camera. She checked its alignment against the illustration in the journal. She made a slight adjustment. When the image in the camera and the image in the journal were identical, she snapped the shutter.

She pushed the review button on the camera so they could see the photograph she just took. And there it was, exactly the same as the illustration in the journal.

And Hannah's heart sunk. Apart from being identical, the two images were meaningless. She was no closer to deciphering the map than before.

"I thought this would be the answer," she said, staring at the camera in disbelief. "It all made such sense…"

Clooney rested a reassuring hand on her shoulder. "The answer will come. You'll figure it out. You are smart. Smarter than anyone I know. Perhaps just let it go for now."

She looked at him. Let it go? That was about the worst possible thing he could have said in that moment. Henri had been kidnapped, and he needed Hannah to decipher this map. There was no time to let anything go.

As her frustration mounted and the voice in her head became more outraged and insistent, the familiarity of it suddenly reminded her of another conversation—with Henri, long ago, during the first archaeological dig she had ever helped him with.

They were working at a site in Jerusalem. It was Hannah's first day on the job. Henri explained the site they were excavating had been the location of several battles, and there had once been a church, a mosque, and a synagogue, each in their own day, though not even a foundation stone remained standing from any one of them.

Henri had put Hannah on sifting duty because he knew sifting would be fun, and he hoped to snare Hannah's interest as soon as possible. Hannah's job was to scoop mud from a bucket and spread it across a sifting screen. Then she sprayed the mud with a hose, washing it away until only solid items remained. Sifting was an exciting duty because with the least amount of work, you had a chance to uncover genuine treasures and artifacts hidden from human eyes for centuries, even eons.

Within five minutes of beginning her task, Hannah's hose had a revealed fragment of green glass with bubbles still in it. Thinking it a broken beer bottle, she was prepared to throw it away until Henri stopped her. Holding an umbrella above them both to shade their view from the sun, he pointed to the glass in her hand. "See those bubbles, deep in the glass?"

She nodded.

"That means it's old. Very old. When they used to make glass long ago, they couldn't get the fires as hot as we can today and so little bubbles formed in the glass. This, Hannah, is a genuine artifact."

Later that afternoon she uncovered a small chunk of pink plaster, which Henri said came from a mosque that once stood on this site. And then, just before day's end, she discovered the most interesting find of all: A copper medallion, tarnished green with age. The medallion was a cross. But instead of being T-shaped, each arm of the cross was equal in size and shape, giving it the overall appearance of a square with four identical, smaller crosses around it.

"It's the symbol for the Order of the Holy Sepulcher," said Henry with interest. "Left behind by the Knights of the Holy

Sepulcher when they ruled Jerusalem. Probably from around 1100 CE or so."

Hannah stared in awe. She was holding a piece of history. Someone, a real person, and possibly an actual knight, held this very object in their hand nearly nine-hundred years ago. Bewitched with wonder, she quietly turned the object in her hand, holding it up to the light.

"I believe you have caught the bug," winked Henri. "I can see it in your eyes."

"What bug?"

"The archaeology bug!"

When Hannah left the dig site that evening, she couldn't wait to return. All night she thought about the things she had seen and found and touched with her own hands.

When she and Henri returned the next day, however, they found the site had been demolished. Everything was upturned. The pulleys were shattered and tools tossed about. Hannah was speechless.

"Who would do this?" she whispered.

Her grandfather sighed. "Many people, actually. More than you might think."

"But why?"

Henri stroked his bushy white mustache, appearing to search for an explanation. "It's like this," Henri said. "Jerusalem is a land of many cultures, many religions, all fighting for ownership of one place. Something as simple as a coin, which we call an artifact, could be used as evidence to disprove another man's beliefs."

"How so?"

"Well, one man looks at this coin, and he says, You see! This coin, which has the image of our ancient king printed alongside a date, it's proof that my people were here first! And therefore we have most right to be here! And another man disagrees, or worse, he fears it may be true, and so what does he do?"

"He destroys the dig site and all the evidence in it," said Hannah, looking about at the destruction.

Henri handed her the umbrella as though it were a token of some initiation. "Hannah, if you stay here long enough, you'll see. This is all part of being an archaeologist in Jerusalem. You must let it go."

"I will not!" she yelled, storming away. She immediately began righting tipped objects and cleaning up the mess. "I will not let it go, and stop saying I should."

Because that's what they said at the funeral.

Because that's what they said when she'd cried.

Because no matter what they said, Hannah feared *letting go* might be the same as forgetting.

Then she saw the sadness in Henri's eyes, and she suddenly felt ashamed of her outburst. She wanted to apologize, but couldn't bring herself to speak. And she didn't need to because Henri understood. He always understood.

Her grandfather had taken her in his arms. "He was my son, too, you know. When your father died in that fire, I lost someone as well. I know how it feels, how much pain one heart can feel."

She sniffed against his shoulder. "Then how do you do it? How do you say goodbye when it hurts so bad?"

"I let it in," he said. "I let it in."

He pulled back from the hug. He strode to the table, which had been flipped on its side. He scouted about in the dirt and then bent to retrieve the medallion. The one Hannah had found the day before. He strung it on a leather cord.

"Here," he said, placing it around her neck. "Worse things have happened at this location than the disappearance of one cross. I want you to wear this."

"But it's a cross, Henri. We are Jewish. How can I wear a cross?"

"We are archaeologists!" he said. "We seek only the truth! Remember that Hannah. No matter our beliefs, it is our job to remember what others have forgotten."

"Hannah?" said Clooney, still standing on the shore of the Dead Sea. "Are you all right?"

She nodded, stroking the copper medallion around her neck.

"They are inviting us to their fire," said Clooney.

Hannah turned and saw most of the campers were now gathered around a fire, several of them enthusiastically waving her over.

The moment she and Clooney entered their circle she was patted on the back, and everyone announced his or her name.

Hannah counted eight adults, six children, and three or four in between. She had no idea which were parents and which were friends, or who might be related to who. It was all pleasantly mixed up.

"Do you two need a place to camp?" asked a friendly woman with a child resting on her lap.

"We do," said Hannah.

"Do you have blankets? Any gear for sleeping?"

Reluctantly, Hannah shook her head, fearing the woman might ridicule her for traveling unprepared.

But the woman just said, "No problem. We can set you up in the kid's tent. That ok with you guys?" she asked the little ones, and they all yelled hooray.

The woman's name was Cara. She said they were all touring Israel by bicycle for the next six weeks. Even the little ones rode. All four families had been resting and camping here at the Dead Sea for the last few days.

"So are you guys travelling on your own or what?" asked Cara.

Hannah and Clooney shared a look.

"Yes," confessed Hannah, uncertain how Cara would respond. But Cara just said cool, that's cool, she was hitchhiking through Central America when she was their age, or maybe a little older, but man was that ever amazing, to be cruising through Costa Rica in the nineties before tourism ruined it and anyway, Israel is way safer for young travelers, and are they hungry?

"Very!" said Hannah and Clooney in unison.

They were each given bowls of steaming rice with lentils. No one ever asked Hannah why she was without her parents or where she was headed. Everyone just seemed to accept she and Clooney were part of the family for the night, and that was that.

After dinner, the tall skinny man with the dreadlocks and long beard began to play his flute. Everyone called him Gumbo. At first, Hannah thought he looked a bit scary, especially when she saw the tattoos on his neck, but he turned out to be the silliest person she had ever met—more like a child than an adult.

"Gumbo! Do your eyes!" yelled the children. "Do your eyes!"

And Gumbo would cross his eyes until his pupils nearly disappeared and hop about and even do somersaults, all the while playing his flute. The children rolled with laughter.

Then a young man whose entire back was covered in colorful tattoos fetched a guitar from his tent. He strummed and sang, and others sang along and tapped at little handheld drums and even cooking pots, whatever they could find to keep a beat. Hannah and Clooney were given pots as well, and they sat beside one another as they played.

The first tune was a Christian hymn. Hannah knew the melody but not the words, so she just hummed along. Next they sang an old Hebrew song, which Hannah did know. This time she sang. Hannah loved to sing.

After the song came a short lull, and everyone gazed quietly at the fire until Clooney asked aloud, "So how does one become a hippy?"

Everyone laughed and clapped, as though this were the best question on earth, and Hannah explained to their new friends that Clooney had a certain fascination with American culture. Any tips they could offer would be appreciated.

In response, the guitarist with the tattoos started up a catchy tune, saying, "This one's for you, Clooney. It's a Sufi song. The Sufis are Muslims who love to sing and dance. You know this one?"

"Of course!" Clooney jumped from his seat and launched into a dance, singing at the top of his voice. Everyone shouted him on, and then Gumbo jumped up and did a wild jig alongside him. Hannah was surprised to discover Clooney had an amazing voice, and he belted it out with genuine passion.

When the singing finished, a young woman with cropped blonde hair continued tapping quietly at a small drum, lost in thought, all the while watching Hannah and Clooney across the fire. Eventually she set the drum down and said, "You guys should be, like, the poster children for peace."

"What does that mean?" asked Hannah.

The woman said, "You do realize your people and his people are, like, basically at war?"

Hannah glanced at Clooney. As usual, he shrugged.

"Seriously, you two are great," the woman said. "I love you two. You're a Palestinian kid with an Aeropostale T-shirt, sitting beside a Jewish girl with a cross around her neck... you guys are just awesome."

And everyone chimed in. "We love you Hannah and Clooney!"

And then the guitarist tossed a small stick into the fire and said, "War sucks, man."

And then Cara, who still had a child in her lap, she said, "You got that right. War sucks."

Caught up in the moment, a third man threw his arms in the air and shook his head like a dog and howled, "Waaaar suuuucks!"

A chant started up, and everyone pounded the earth like a drum, singing, "War sucks! War sucks! War sucks!"

Gumbo ripped off his tank top and cried, "To the sea!" And everyone, Hannah and Clooney included, began shouting like banshees as they sprinted down to the water and jumped in with all their clothes on.

As their excitement died down, and they all lay floating on their backs in the dark cool of the Dead Sea, someone suggested they form a single line and all hold hands, each person to the next, and that nobody speak, and in the silence of the desert they all drifted and hovered, and sometimes someone would pretend to snore or whisper, *War sucks, man,* and a bit of laughter would flare up, and then it would subside, all of them together, floating quietly beneath the soft smooth light of the moon.

Cara had given Hannah and Clooney dry clothes to sleep in. They spent the night in the tent beside six squirming kids, but they had little to complain about. It was safe and cozy,

and when they woke, several of the adults were already preparing breakfast over campstoves. Nothing was discussed,
it was just assumed Hannah and Clooney would be joining the meal and were given bowls of oatmeal along with
the other children. Hannah wondered if anyone would even
bother to comment if she were to hop on a bicycle and join
their tour.

When she finished, Hannah helped with the wash up.

"Where are you going?" asked Clooney, spooning up a
second bowl of oatmeal.

"I will be back in a minute. I just want to see something,"
said Hannah.

She took her camera and journal down to the shore. She
sat crosslegged on the salt beach and began to think. She
looked at the journal in her lap. Then the camera. She still
felt Henri had been directing her to use her camera, and the
"magic eye" was his clue. But how did it all fit together?

She opened the journal to the first illustration, the one of
the Dead Sea. Beneath it were the numbers her grandfather
had written.

f.4   125   400

Hannah recalled her first photography lesson. She and
Henri were sitting on a stone wall overlooking the hills east
of Jerusalem. He passed her the camera. "This is now yours,"
he said. "I am giving it to you. On one condition…"

Hannah accepted the camera, turning it over in her hands.
"What's the condition?"

"You must learn how to use it. Every dial. Every button. Every setting. A camera is like an enchanted box. With it, you can capture the world," and then he added with meaning, "Or even recreate it..."

Henri pointed to the various settings on the camera. He explained that she could control the exposure, or how much light entered the camera, by making three adjustments. The first adjustment was called the 'aperture.' The second was called the 'shutter speed.' And the last was called 'ISO.' It took some practice to work out what each setting did, but in the end, she found the camera was indeed like an enchanted box and entirely under her control. All she had to do was adjust the three settings.

The *three numbers* that affected the camera's exposure...

Could it be that simple?

She looked at the numbers in the journal again.

f.4　125　400

What if she were to insert each of those three numbers into each of the camera's three settings? At the very least, it was worth a try.

She started with the aperture. She set it to four. Easy.

Next was shutter speed, which she set to 1/125 of a second.

Last, she set the ISO to 400. She looked through the viewfinder, composing it to match the illustration in the journal. She snapped the shutter.

She pushed the button to review the photograph and nearly dropped the camera.

"Clooney!" she yelled from the shore, her eyes riveted on the photograph. "Clooney, come quick!"

He sprinted over, sliding to halt beside her. He glanced over her shoulder, staring in awe at the photograph displayed on her camera.

"How did you do that?"

She smiled.

The image on the camera was identical to the illustration in the journal and also the photograph she took last night. Except for one detail. Rising up from the Dead Sea, one of the saltiest bodies of water on earth, there appeared the ghostly image of a pillar. As though an ancient marble column had once existed in that place and was now slowly returning to view.

As Hannah marveled at the image, she actually felt the hairs rise on her neck. Her pulse quickened. This was her first real glimpse of Julien's sorcery in action—or any magic for that matter—and it was beautiful.

"I can't believe it's this easy," she said. "Each of these numbers beneath the illustrations. They are camera settings for the exposure. A particular exposure that deciphers Julien's illustrations. Like a code."

"What do you mean deciphers?" asked Clooney. "Are you saying you understand what the image means?"

"Of course. I see a pillar rising from the salty sea. A *Pillar of Salt...*"

"You mean *the* Pillar of Salt? The tourist site? We saw signs for that place all along the highway."

"It is where we are supposed to go. Hidden in each illustration will be a clue to the next. All we have to do is locate the place each illustration was drawn, decipher it with the proper exposure on this camera, and follow the clues like bread crumbs back to King Solomon's treasure."

"But this is amazing! How did your grandfather ever figure this out? And how did Julien even create the clues in the first place?"

"I have no idea. But I'm not surprised. Julien Dubuisson was supposedly a sorcerer. And Henri is a master at cracking codes. He has spent years on this. And fortunately for us, he left the key to decoding each illustration right here in this journal."

Hannah wondered, was this why Henri had given her the camera so long ago? Had he always intended to include her on this strange, dangerous journey?

"The Pillar of Salt should be just down the highway," said Clooney. "Let's get started!"

Hannah and Clooney changed out of their borrowed clothing, even though Hannah's dress from last night's swim was still a little damp. They said goodbye to Gumbo and Cara and the wonderful people they had met and hiked up to the highway.

The Pillar of Salt wasn't far away. Cara figured twenty kilometers at most. She suggested they just hitchhike it and would probably arrive within the hour.

Hannah and Clooney stood on the side of the highway, the mountains of Jordan at their back, and waited for a car to come by. The sun was already hot on their skin. A car approached, and Clooney put out his thumb. The car zipped past without a glance.

"Here comes another," said Hannah. "Try again."

Clooney stuck out his thumb, and this time the driver looked in their direction, but still roared by.

"Is there a trick to it?" he asked.

"I have no idea. I have never hitchhiked before."

The third and the fourth cars actually sped up when they saw Clooney's thumb jutting in the air.

"Perhaps we should dance," he suggested.

Hannah gave him a look.

"I am serious. Let's give it try it." Clooney pushed his giant sunglasses higher on his nose and began to clap a rhythm above his head, wagging his hips side to side and singing in his loudest voice, "Hannah loves to dance! Oh yes, she dances all day long! Hannah loves to—"

"I will not dance on the road."

"Hannah, Hannah, Hannah, she does not look like a banana! She dances like a—"

"You are wasting your time."

"Here comes a car! Quickly! Join me!"

She saw the approaching car. Before she could say another word, Clooney grabbed both her hands and pulled her into a dance step, and Hannah gave in, and found herself grooving on the side of the highway to the stupidest song she had ever heard.

"Hannah, Hannah, Hannah, she comes from Indiana!"

As the car drew nearer they heard the beat of loud music. The whole car was rattling with it. Without breaking rhythm, Clooney waved his arms and the car immediately slowed and then veered across the highway, pulling to a halt beside them. It was a Palestinian family packed to the gills inside a battered little sedan. Hannah peeked inside and counted seven people stuffed in there. The driver was a young man, and an elderly man sat in the passenger seat beside him. In the back seat were three women in burkas, which were like black gowns that covered them from head to toe, with only a small screen to view out. Squished between them were two small children. A boy and a girl.

Clooney leaned into the driver's-side window and spoke in brisk Arabic, and seconds later they were piling into the backseat of the sedan, everyone greeting them with a lively, "As-salam alaykum!"

Clooney was shoved up against the door, his shoulder pressed to the window. Hannah was literally sitting on one woman's lap. The woman casually wrapped her arms around Hannah's waist like a seatbelt, as though they did this all the time, and asked Clooney in Arabic if Hannah was comfortable.

"Very. Thank you," she said.

The young driver cranked the music back on—Arabic pop music, inexplicably loud—and happily sped onto the highway. Above the blaring of music, the inquisitive passengers fired questions at Clooney. Hannah had no idea what they discussed.

At one point, he explained, "They're going on a family picnic. And they've invited us along."

"Will they be passing the Pillar of Salt?"

He asked.

"They said they can even stop and picnic there if we wish."

The car vibrated and pounded to the beat of the music, and the woman behind Hannah tapped both feet, and Hannah went up and down. Up and down. It was difficult to describe how much Hannah enjoyed this family. She didn't understand a word they said and hadn't even seen all their faces, but their joy was infectious, much like the American campers of last night, and when the woman's arms squeezed Hannah tight and began rocking side-to-side, Hannah leaned with her, feeling the music. The beat of different lives, moving as one.

They passed a road sign for the Pillar of Salt. Four kilometers further. Moments later the sedan pulled into a parking lot with signs for restrooms and gift shops. Tour buses idled on the searing hot asphalt and red-faced Europeans purchased sunhats and bottled water.

Their Palestinian hosts spread a blanket on the grass near the parking lot. Out came the food, boxes of juice, napkins, dishes, wooden utensils. Apart from the bread and olives, Hannah didn't recognize much of what they ate. One of the women in burkas, who sounded quite old by her voice, kept pressing bits of dried mango at Hannah, and she gratefully accepted.

The young driver was speaking with Clooney. Hannah learned she had been sitting in the lap of the driver's wife.

Also in the car were their two children, the driver's sister, and both their parents.

"What is he saying now?" asked Hannah.

"He is talking about the Pillar of Salt," said Clooney.

The young man pointed to the ridge on the mountain high above them, and Clooney translated. "He says it's that rock, right there. That huge orange stone that appears to have split off from the rest."

Hannah opened her journal to the second illustration, and there it was. The Pillar of Salt. Julien's illustration was upside down, of course, but there was no mistaking the same giant stone, splintering off from the ridge. They had found the second of the map's locations.

Clooney continued to translate while the young man told the story of this site and why it was called the Pillar of Salt, even though the rock was neither a pillar, nor made of salt. It originated from the story of Lot. According to the story, Lot was a man who supposedly lived long ago. And despite being a good man, he lived in an evil city, which was about to be destroyed by angels. So the angels gave Lot fair warning, instructing him to leave with his family at once. And no matter what, said the angels, Lot should never look back at the city.

As Lot and his family fled into the desert and the city was destroyed, Lot's wife turned back with a look of longing for her old home. She was instantly transformed into a pillar of salt.

Of course, this natural rock formation had no real connection to the story, but it nevertheless became a place for tourists to pose for photos, purchase water and postcards, and read a bit of history.

"I know that story," said Hannah.

"But it is from the Koran. The holy book of Islam," said Clooney. "How do you know the story of Lot?"

"Because it also comes from a Jewish book called the Tanakh. Christians told the same story in the Old Testament of the bible."

"You mean Islam and Judaism and Christianity share the same stories?" he asked in surprise.

"I guess so," she said, shrugging. "And why not? Islam, Christianity, and Judaism all share the same patriarch."

Hannah knew that all three religions traced their origins to one man, a man named Abraham. Still, it was fun discovering that she and Clooney had more in common than she first assumed.

Hannah opened the journal again, studying the illustration. She was trying to figure out where exactly Julien would have stood when he traced it with the camera obscura.

She wandered over to a handrail and stopped. Beside her was an interpretive placard for tourists. It was a large photograph of the ridge before her with a little arrow labeling the famed Pillar of Salt.

Hannah composed the camera and found it lined up with the illustration. This time, she inserted the following three numbers to open the encoded exposure:

f.16   1200   1200

She snapped the photo.

"What do you see?" Clooney asked at her side.

The photograph showed the Pillar of Salt. It was identical to Julien's illustration, except this time a single word appeared written across the huge orange stone. The word was:

Khātim

Hannah was baffled. *Khātim?* She had no idea what it meant. How would she ever—

"Emblem," said Clooney, peeking over her shoulder.

"What did you say?"

"Emblem," he repeated, as if everyone knew that. "*Khātim* means emblem. Or symbol. It's Arabic."

"Really? You know this word?"

He shrugged.

So *Khātim* means emblem, or symbol. But Hannah still didn't know what to do with it. Were they supposed to find an emblem of some kind? Draw an emblem? Julien had clearly put the clue there on purpose, but left no further hint to help find the next location.

She opened the journal and flipped through the pages until she found the third illustration. The third point on the map.

It was an enormous block of carved stone. Part of a wall, by the look of it. It was rectangular and blockish and, well… it was a block of stone. It gave no hint where it might be. And unless one has been to Israel and hunted about its countless ruins as Hannah had done with her grandfather, it's hard to appreciate just how many large blocks of carved stone exist in that land. They are everywhere. The cities are literally built of such blocks. How would they ever find this particular one?

"Well, we have the word *Khātim*, or emblem, but no idea what to do next," she said. "I think we are stuck."

Despondent, Hannah rested her camera on the interpretive placard beside her. In addition to pointing out the pillar to curious tourists, the placard told the story of Lot and his wife in eight different languages. Hannah glanced at the English version. The first paragraph began with the following verse from the Christian bible:

> *"But his wife looked back from behind him, and she became a pillar of salt."*

The placard then described the history behind this verse and how it led to the naming of this location.

Hannah paused and read it again. *But his wife looked back from behind him...*

Slowly, Hannah turned around, looking behind her. And there was the road, leading back the way she had come.

"Jerusalem," she whispered to herself.

"What's that?" asked Clooney.

"That's where our next clue is hiding," she said. "*Jerusalem.*"

The Palestinian family was from Jerusalem and was happy to drive Hannah and Clooney back with them. Hannah resumed her position on the woman's lap. Clooney pressed himself against the driver's-side door, jabbering to any and all.

The little girl beside Hannah engaged her in a sort of hand game. It involved the two of them intertwining their fingers to make animal shapes, birds and lions, dogs, a two-headed giant, a man with a hat. The girl asked to see the journal lying in Hannah's lap.

Hannah opened it. There seemed no harm in sharing the journal here. The girl pointed to the illustrations as Hannah flipped through the pages, asking in English, "What's this?" and "What's this?" Hannah had no idea what to say. So she simply turned the pages, letting the girl browse until they came to the third illustration. The carved block of stone. Hannah found herself gazing at it again, wondering if some further clue lay hidden within the illustration.

Knowing the block lay in Jerusalem certainly tightened the net, but there would still be countless walls to search, countless carved blocks within each.

"What's this?" asked the girl, pointing to the illustration.

"Stone," Hannah answered in her best teacher's voice. "It's called a *stone*. Can you say—"

"What's this?" the girl said again, pointing to the same image, more insistently this time. Hannah looked closer and realized the girl wasn't actually pointing to the stone. She was pointing at something beside the stone in the picture. Something small, like a tiny object that had been shoved into the crack between this stone block and the next. In fact, it looked just like…

"Clooney, is that what I think it is?" She handed him the journal, pointing out what the girl had found.

"It looks like a folded piece of paper," he said, "or a note that someone tried to hide in the wall."

How did Hannah miss this? It was so obvious now that it had been pointed out. And she knew exactly where it was.

"This carved block is from the Western Wall," she said. And it made perfect sense because the Western Wall was built on the same site as King Solomon's temple.

Solomon was the first Jewish king to build a temple there. It was destroyed, then rebuilt. Then destroyed again, and rebuilt a last time by King Herod. But when the Romans invaded Jerusalem nearly two thousand years ago, they pulled everything down and scattered the huge blocks. Of the temple that was once the Jews' holiest site, only one wall was left standing. It came to be called the Western Wall, and for the last five hundred years, Jews had gathered before this wall to pray.

Over time, an unusual tradition developed. Those who came to pray at the Western Wall wrote their prayers upon paper, like a secret note to God, and then pressed the folded message into the seams between the stones of the wall. Today, more than a million notes a year were tucked into the Western Wall. So many notes that they had to be regularly cleared out to make room for more.

Hannah remembered the first time she had seen the Western Wall. It was such an odd sight, that towering battlement with bits of paper of every imaginable colour literally bursting from its seams. The tradition of hiding notes to God would have been the same in Julien's day.

"Next stop," said Hannah. "The Jewish Quarter of Jerusalem."

The car dropped them off outside Zion Gate, and it was a short walk into the Jewish Quarter. They passed through the newly installed security gate, complete with metal detectors and soldiers with machine guns. After a brief moment of anxiety, Hannah passed through the checkpoint. The soldiers had their hands full with the line up. They simply peeked at the camera in her backpack and handed it back, saying nothing more. Moments later she and Clooney entered a large plaza, fronted by a tremendous stone rampart. The Western Wall.

Even from a distance Hannah could see the countless bits of colored paper outlining the lower stones like grout. There were hundreds of people before the wall. Many pressed their foreheads to the huge stones, their mouths whispering silent prayers. Others read aloud from the holy Tanakh. Most of the men present were orthodox Jews in their identical black suits. Seeing hundreds of men together in one place, all dressed the same, always reminded Hannah of an M.C. Escher picture.

The wall was sectioned off, so that men prayed on the left and women on the right. "We'll have to split up," she said.

"Remember, we are looking for a carved block that is shaped just like this." She pointed to the illustration in the journal.

Clooney tapped the side of his head, assuring her that he had memorized the image, and then went left. Hannah kept the journal before her and joined the women praying on the right. She went straight to the wall and began her search. The gender partition wouldn't have been here in Julien's day, so she had just as much chance of finding the stone as Clooney.

It didn't take long. Over the last two hundred years, the blocks hadn't changed, and within a few minutes Hannah had found the stone. There were far more notes in the seams now than when Julien had drawn his illustration, but she was definitely, without a doubt, standing before the same stone he had drawn.

She checked the numbers Henri had written beneath the illustration.

$$f2.2 \quad 500 \quad 100$$

She adjusted the settings on her camera to match. She snapped the photo. She took a step back from the crowd and glanced left and right to ensure no one else was looking.

She pressed the review button and looked at the photograph.

This was the most interesting one yet. There was the carved block, same as in the illustration. Beneath the image of the block appeared a horizontal line, as though Julien had underlined it with a ghostly marking pen. But there was more. Beneath the line, he had placed an arrow pointing down.

And beneath the arrow, one word: *Sulaymāni*.

Hannah didn't even need to ask Clooney this time. She knew *Sulaymāni* was the Arabic word for "Solomon."

Khātim Sulaymāni. Which was the same as "Emblem + Solomon."

So they were looking for Solomon's emblem. Got it. She supposed this meant the hidden treasure would have a special mark, or symbol, to show whom it belonged to. That seemed reasonable to Hannah. She left the women's prayer area and waved her arms till she had Clooney's attention.

He came running over. "Did you find it?"

She nodded. "We're looking for Solomon's emblem."

"Can I have a look?"

They studied the photo together, trying to puzzle out the rest of the clues. Clooney agreed it looked like Julien had underlined the block of stone and then added beneath it an arrow pointing down.

"Could Julien be saying the treasure is under the wall?" asked Clooney.

"Of course!" she replied. "We are standing before the last remaining wall of King Solomon's temple. And this clue says the emblem marking his treasure is just beneath."

"But how do we get under the wall?" asked Clooney, glancing up at its great height.

Hannah pointed to a vending booth. "We buy a ticket," she said.

"A ticket?"

She nodded. "To enter the tunnels beneath. They run the length of the wall. All we need is a ticket, and we can take a guided tour."

They purchased their tickets and five minutes later were joining a group of tourists out front of the entrance leading beneath the Western Wall. A tour guide soon introduced herself and began by explaining a bit of the tunnel's history.

"If you will all follow me," the guide said, "we will now descend the first flight of steps and begin our tour beneath the Western Wall, the last remaining wall of King Solomon's temple."

As they started down into the murky depths of the tunnel, Clooney suddenly halted on the steps, staring wild-eyed at Hannah, "The Emblem of Solomon," he said.

"Right," she replied. "Solomon's emblem. That is what we're looking for."

He shook his head, as though he'd just realized something. "How did I miss this?"

"Miss what?" demanded Hannah.

"The word Khātim," he said. "It means emblem, or symbol. But it can also be translated as *seal*."

"The *Seal of Solomon*? You mean..." Hannah couldn't believe what he was saying. "You mean *the* Seal of Solomon? The famous ring worn by Solomon himself?"

Clooney said, "It's one of the greatest legends in Islam. I knew it all sounded familiar. I should have realized right away."

"Hang on," said Hannah, charging back up the stairs toward the surface until her phone had reception. She did an Internet search for *Seal of Solomon*.

Instantly, page after page of information popped up. She scrolled through the browser, astounded at how many articles and websites were dedicated to this topic.

1. "Understanding the Seal of Solomon"
2. *"Khātim Sulaymāni* in Islamic Lore"
3. "Ten Things You Didn't Know About The Seal Of Solomon"

The list went on. She couldn't believe it.

Hannah needed look no further than the first page to discover the *Seal of Solomon* was indeed a legendary ring worn by King Solomon. The ring was supposedly imprinted with the name of God and set with four jewels, which were given to King Solomon by angels. And most interesting of all, the ring was considered the source of King Solomon's wisdom and even gave him magical powers.

Hannah was thunderstruck. This changed everything. Absolutely everything. The map. The treasure. Nothing was as it seemed.

"Clooney," she said, her voice trembling with excitement. "We are not looking for King Solomon's treasure."

He met her eyes, slowly nodding in understanding.

"We are hunting for the legendary ring of King Solomon. A magic ring."

"This is amazing," he said. "You know what, Hannah?"

She shook her head.

"You," he said, "are more fun than any girl I have ever met in my life."

She chuckled.

"And this should *definitely* be a movie," he said. "And you and I are *definitely* going to be the stars."

But Hannah was distracted. She was still thinking about the Seal of Solomon, and that Henri must have known. As Henri plodded through the map, one location at a time, he would have learned that the map led to wisdom, a magic ring of wisdom, and not the famed horde of temple gold. But did the Cancellarii know this as well?

Hannah quickly scanned the rest of the article.

The ring was made from a mixture of iron and brass. A six-pointed star had been pressed into the metal, alongside the 'Most High' name of God. In addition to wisdom, the ring gave Solomon power over the four elements and genies as well. The Seal of Solomon, the article read, was primarily an Islamic legend. But Hannah was surprised to discover the legend occurred in ancient Hebraic and Christian lore too. It appeared all three of Jerusalem's main religions could be traced back to King Solomon and tied together with the legend of this very ring.

Hannah looked at Clooney. For the second time that day his differing background, having been raised as a Muslim, had given them the key information they needed to decipher the map. And she thought she was the archaeologist here…

"You know," she said. "We make a good team."

"Which reminds me. Do you recall an agreement we once had? Something about a kiss?"

"No time for that. Come on, we have a tour to catch!"

They raced down the steps until they reached the cluster of tourists. They were crowded around the guide, who was at that moment pointing to a large block in the wall.

"Over here," their guide was saying, "is the largest stone in the entire wall. It's called the Western Stone. It weighs 520 tons, making it one of the largest blocks of stone ever used in construction. And it was carved and placed here two thousand years *before* the existence of modern machines."

While the woman pointed out other interesting facts about this tremendous stone, Clooney whispered, "Let's see the next illustration. I want to know what we are looking for."

Hannah opened the journal to the fourth image. According to the journal, somewhere down here in this tunnel was another tunnel, leading off from the first. Except this second tunnel appeared blocked off. As though someone had built a wall to prevent passage. Beneath the illustration, in addition to Henri's three numbers, he had scrawled a brief note to himself. He simply wrote: *The cave.*

The cave? The illustration looked nothing like a cave. What was Henri referring to?

As the guide led them deeper into the tunnel, describing points of interest along the way, Hannah used the flashlight on her phone to keep one eye on the journal, checking for anything along the way that matched Julien's illustration.

"Is that it?" asked Clooney.

"Not even close. What about over here?"

"No. That looks more like an ancient toilet."

"Please keep up!" the guide called back to them. The cluster of tourists was now several metres ahead, gathering before a niche in the wall.

"Sorry, coming!" Clooney called back. "We better keep up, or she might throw us off this tour."

When they arrived, Hannah and Clooney found themselves stuck behind the group, unable to see. They could hear the guide's voice describing something on the far side of the tourists.

"Behind me," the guide announced, "was once a tunnel that branched off and led all the way to the Temple Mount, where the arc of the covenant was once kept in King Solomon's temple. The arc was very important to the Jews because it supposedly carried the laws given to Moses by God. As you can see," she continued, "the tunnel has been filled in. It was blocked off about a thousand years ago. But because it was the closest the Jews could get to Solomon's original temple, and the place where the holy arc was kept, many Jews came here to this very place to pray. This place may have had another name long ago, but today," she said, "we simply call it *the cave*."

Clooney nudged Hannah, and she nodded right back.

"Shall we continue?" suggested the guide. "Now down this hall, you will find…"

As the herd of tourists trundled off, eager to keep pace with their guide, Hannah was given her first glimpse of what lay hidden behind them.

And there it was. The cave. Which was no cave at all, really. She was looking upon a second tunnel blocked off with stone.

"This is it!" said Clooney. "Hurry! Before the guide notices we're gone."

Hannah shined her flashlight on the journal. Beneath Julien's illustration, she saw Henri's numbers.

$$f1.8 \quad 100 \quad 6400$$

She adjusted the three settings according to the code. She snapped the photo.

"Bam," said Clooney, gazing at the photo. "There it is. Another arrow."

This arrow was different though. Instead of pointing down, like the arrow in the last photo, this arrow appeared to point directly *into* the photo, away from the viewer, leading them deeper into the tunnel in the picture.

Except there was a wall before them. A wall they could not pass.

"Didn't that woman say this wall was built a thousand years ago?" Hannah asked in confusion.

Clooney nodded. "That would mean it was here when Julien sketched it as well. It doesn't make sense. Why would he create an arrow here, if the tunnel is blocked off?"

"Wait a minute," said Hannah. "What if Julien is simply telling us to follow the tunnel, to go where it goes? And the guide already told us where it goes…"

"It goes to the Temple Mount!" cried Clooney. "You're a genius! Julien is sending us to the Temple Mount. That's where the next clue is hidden! But what's wrong Hannah? You look like you'll be sick."

Hannah looked at him. She opened the journal and showed him the next illustration. It was the image of a gigantic stone sitting in the floor of a shrine. There was only one place this could be.

"The Dome of the Rock," he said. It was the oldest Muslim shrine, sitting right in the middle of the Temple Mount. "It's the next clue. And you aren't allowed inside the Dome of the Rock because…"

"I'm not a Muslim," she said, finishing his sentence.

Just as the Western Wall was an important place of prayer for Jews, the Dome of the Rock was Jerusalem's most sacred shrine for Muslims. They believed their prophet, Muhammad, had ascended to heaven from that very stone, and so they built a gigantic gold-covered dome over the rock to house it.

The Dome was visible from just about every point in Jerusalem. Hannah had seen it from the outside countless times. Her problem was that no non-Muslims were allowed inside. The last time a group of Jewish pilgrims and tourists attempted to enter, the Palestinians protested, and riots broke out. If Hannah tried to enter the Dome of the Rock to photograph the ancient stone, it could get serious, fast.

So how would Hannah decipher the map if she wasn't allowed inside the golden Dome?

"I can see two choices," said Clooney. "First choice, you give up."

"That will not happen."

"Second choice. You let me enter the Dome of the Rock and take the picture of the stone. I'm a Muslim. They won't even blink an eye."

Hannah shook her head. "Henri gave me the map. It's up to me to do this. Besides, you don't even know how to use my camera."

"But you'll never get in. And if you do, you'll probably be arrested. The Temple Mount is patrolled by the Waqf."

"The Waqf? What is that?" she asked.

"They're the Islamic religious authorities in charge of the whole Temple Mount area, which includes the Dome of the Rock. Their job is to make sure people like you don't create trouble."

"Can you sneak me past the Waqf? And get me into the shrine?"

"Hannah, this is serious. If you get caught, they'll bring in the police."

Hannah didn't need Clooney to explain that police meant Andrepont. And Andrepont meant the Cancellarii. Sneaking into the Dome would be both dangerous and tricky.

"There is a third option," said Hannah. "I could ask for Professor Weisman's help. She is an archaeologist at the university. She knows many people. Maybe she can get me into the Dome."

Hannah and Clooney hurried back to the surface. Standing in the plaza before the Western Wall, she called Professor Weisman. Upon hearing Hannah's voice, the professor heaved a sigh of relief. She said Hannah could not imagine how worried she had been. Hannah apologized for their abrupt departure and began to update the professor on their discoveries, when Professor Weisman interrupted her.

"Hannah, we should not discuss any of this on the phone. It is far too dangerous. Come to my office, where we can talk safely." They were about to hang up, when the professor added, "Oh, and Hannah," she said. "Bring the journal…"

Hannah and Clooney took the bus back to the university. They crossed the wide lawn and recognized the same guard, standing like a statue before the building's glass doors, his hands clasped behind his back. He wore the uniform of a security guard and had short brown hair, thin, pale lips, and the shoulders of a bull. As Hannah approached the doors, she noticed him whispering into his radio, just as he had done last time.

Clooney noticed too. "I don't like him, Hannah."

"Neither do I. But I must go up."

"Then I'll wait here," he suggested. "If I notice any trouble, I'll give you a sign." He showed her his slingshot. "If you hear a pebble on your window, that means get out. Trouble is on its way."

Hannah nodded and started through glass doors. She rode the elevator up to the fifth floor and all the while felt a pit in her belly. Like something bad was about to happen.

But as she entered the office, Hannah relaxed. Professor Weisman was like a smile factory, bursting with salutations as she poured cups of steaming tea for the two of them.

Hannah went straight to the window, lifted the blind and saw Clooney on the pavement below. He waved and then saluted her. She waved back and took her seat in the chair opposite Weisman's desk.

"Sorry about running off," Hannah began. "I know you were worried, but I just had to find Henri."

"Of course you did, dear. I am just glad you are safe," said Weisman, patting her hand. "Any news of your grandfather?"

"No," said Hannah. "The Cancellarii still have him. But I learned something important. About the journal, and the map. And I need your help."

"Oh?" said Weisman, taking a sip of tea. "And what did you learn?"

"Well," said Hannah. "Remember how you said the map leads to King Solomon's treasure? A treasure of silver and gold?"

Weisman nodded, eagerly following the conversation.

"It doesn't lead to gold," said Hannah. "It leads to a ring. A magic ring. It's called the Seal of Solomon."

Weisman nearly choked on her tea. "The Seal of Solomon! But how do you know this?"

"It's a long story. But for now, I need your help getting into the Dome of the Rock."

Professor Weisman held up her hands. "Slow down, Hannah! Slow down! The Seal of Solomon? The Dome of the Rock? Do you understand what you are asking? You can't enter the Dome. Even I have never entered."

"Yes, but I thought with the university, and you are an archaeologist, and Henri said you knew practically everyone… Is there nothing you can do to help?"

"Hannah, this is no small task. The Dome of the Rock is completely off limits. And if the Waqf ever found out I had aided your entry… well the consequences for the university would be enormous." Professor Weisman eyed Hannah. "Before I even consider this favour, I would need to know why it's necessary. Why don't you show me the journal? You do have it with you, don't you?"

Weisman took another sip of tea, casually awaiting Hannah's response, but Hannah ignored the question.

"Professor Weisman, I need to ask you something."

The professor sat back in her seat, motioning for Hannah to continue.

"I want to know if you think the Seal of Solomon is real. If it really has magical powers. And if you think this map really leads to it."

"Let me put it this way. I believe your grandfather believed it. And that, dear girl, is proof enough for me. I have known Henri a long time. He wouldn't put his nose into something he did not believe genuine. And the Seal of Solomon, should it prove real, would be far more valuable than any amount of gold. It would in fact be priceless. A treasure greater than any the world has known."

"Greater than 56 billion dollars?" asked Hannah, recalling the figure Weisman had given her on the previous visit.

"Hannah, if the legend of the Seal is true, then the ring contains the wisdom of King Solomon, which no amount of gold can purchase. From an archaeological standpoint, it would be the find of the century."

In her excitement, Professor Weisman went on to explain that all three of Israel's religions—Judaism, Islam, and Christianity—told the story of King Solomon's wisdom and described the ring which the angels had given him. It was said that only Solomon was worthy of bearing the ring because such power would be devastating if it fell into the wrong hands. And so safeties were created to keep the ring safe and to prevent evildoers from ever acquiring it.

"But that is nonsense, naturally," said Weisman, waving the notion away. "It is only a fool who fears power. And such fools, of course, should never have power in the first place."

"If this ring is as powerful as you say," said Hannah, "perhaps it is wise to be careful."

"Wise!" barked Weisman, surprising Hannah with his abruptness. "Do not confuse wisdom with fear."

"I am only saying there might be a reason King Solomon hid the ring and kept it safe from the world. Henri always said, 'power follows wisdom.'"

"I disagree," Weisman said outright. "I would say the opposite. Wisdom follows power. Think of it this way. Power is not only in ancient rings. It exists in many things." She rummaged through the drawer of her desk and suddenly removed a pistol, which she pointed at Hannah. "A gun, for example."

Hannah, who generally got along with everyone, was not used to having pistols aimed at her. She gulped.

"So you see, dear Hannah. I now have the power to take your life. You, in return, will give me the journal, which will lead me to a ring of unfathomable wisdom. Bringing us back to my point. *Wisdom follows power…*"

Hannah felt glued to her chair, unable to breathe.

"You are Cancellarii," whispered Hannah with the shock of realization. "You are the Grand Chancellor! I saw you at the airport, in the back of the sedan. That was you who set the motorcyclist after me. You who has been following me all along."

Weisman cocked the pistol. "The journal, dear girl. Believe me when I say I do not wish to use this. But I will if I must."

Slowly, Hannah dug a book from her backpack. She placed it face down upon the desk. She pushed it across. Weisman retrieved the book without taking her eyes from Hannah and placed it into her drawer and shut it.

"Thank you, Hannah, you have been most helpful," she said. "And now to finish this business."

Weisman pressed a button on her office phone. "Will you please send Mr. Jurowitz up to my office? I need him immediately."

Moments later, the professor's door opened, and Hannah recognized the same security guard from before. "Yes, Professor?" said Jurowitz, eyeing Hannah with disdain.

"Mr. Jurowitz, I am happy to say we are now in possession of the item we've long sought."

"We have the old man's journal?" he said.

"We do. But unfortunately we now have a second Dubuisson as well," she said, indicating Hannah. "Tie this girl up and take her to the warehouse. We will keep her hidden along with Henri until this is over. And then we will decide what to do with the two of them."

"My pleasure," said Mr. Jurowitz, stepping toward Hannah.

In that instant, there was a crashing sound, and a rock burst through the window. Bits of glass shattered across the desk, and Weisman turned in surprise. Hannah yanked the umbrella from her backpack and swung it at Weisman's hand. The pistol flew from her grip, skittering across the floor. Hannah took a second swing at Mr. Jurowitz and he jumped back from the blow. Instead of swinging again, she reached for the doorknob and charged out the door, sliding to a halt in the hallway beyond.

She couldn't believe it. Standing at the end of the hall was Inspector Andrepont, appearing equally surprised to see her. They faced off, each eyeing the other, and then Andrepont drew a gun from his jacket and fired…

… at Mr. Jurowitz, who was sneaking up behind Hannah. The security guard leapt back into the office to avoid further gunfire, and Andrepont met Hannah's eyes.

"Run Hannah!" he yelled. "You must run!"

She spun and dashed down the hall in the opposite direction. The elevator doors were open, and she leapt inside, punching the button for the first floor. And as she waited for the doors to close, she heard more gunfire in the hall, two different guns this time. The doors finally closed, and Hannah threw herself against the back wall, breathing hard as the elevator descended.

When she reached the bottom floor and the doors opened, Clooney was standing there, eyes wide. "I saw Andrepont heading into the elevator! Did you see him? I tried to warn you with my slingshot!"

"No time to talk! This way!" The two sprinted out the glass doors, across the lawn and onto the first bus to the Old City of Jerusalem.

They entered the Old City through the Damascus Gate. The sights and smells of the Muslim Quarter once again blasted Hannah back in time. Clooney led the way down the main alley. On the right was a café with two tables out front, and men smoking shisha and drinking coffee. There were orange crates stacked higher than Hannah on either side of the café's arched entrance, and Clooney pulled her inside, sitting her down at a table. The proprietor glanced their way, and Clooney raised two fingers, ordering them each a tea.

Clooney glanced at the patrons of nearby tables, making sure no one was listening.

"We can talk here," he said. "We should be safe."

"I don't want to be safe here," she replied. "I want to go to the Dome of the Rock. Right now. There are no other options. I have to reach the next point and photograph the rock."

"Hannah, you don't even have the journal. You said the professor took it, when she pulled the gun on—" Clooney stopped short as Hannah lifted the journal from her backpack and displayed it upon the café table.

"Wrong," grinned Hannah. "I gave her my copy of *An Illustrated Guidebook To Israel's Historic Sites*. Clooney, we can still do this. You and I can do this, I know we can."

Clooney looked at the journal. He looked at Hannah. "Listen, you know I like to joke around, right? I like to have fun. But this time, no joking. This is for real. You cannot enter the Dome of the Rock. It is simply not possible."

Hannah stood up, preparing to the leave the café. "Then I will go alone."

"Hannah!" he pulled her back to her seat. "Listen to me! The Waqf will catch you, and when they do, it will be trouble. Big trouble."

"If you are scared just say so."

"Of course I am scared! But that isn't the problem."

"I will wear a disguise."

"And if your disguise fails? I don't think you understand the risks, Hannah. If I thought there was a way, believe me, I would help you with this. Why must you always be so stubborn?"

"Stubborn? My grandfather has been kidnapped! The Cancellarii will not stop chasing me, or you for that matter, until they have Solomon's ring. I see no other choice.

"There is one other choice," said Clooney.

Hannah waited for him to speak.

"Let me enter the Dome," he said. "I can take the picture."

"I already told you. You don't know how to use my camera."

"Then teach me," he said. "Teach me, Hannah."

Hannah opened the journal and searched for the exposure settings Clooney would need to photograph inside the Dome. Henri had listed the following three numbers beneath the illustration:

$$f.8 \quad 80 \quad 600$$

Hannah set the exposure and handed the camera to Clooney.

"This is how you turn the camera on," she explained. "I've set the exposure so all you need to do is press this button here. That's what takes the picture."

"Nothing more? This is easy."

"And of course," she added, "you'll need to match the illustration in the journal to your view through the camera. Just don't change any of the settings and it should work. I hope."

She handed him the journal. "Do not lose this."

He smiled. "It will never leave my sight. I promise."

It was not that Hannah didn't trust Clooney. But the idea of giving her camera and the journal over to *anyone* made her very nervous.

"All the same," she said. "I want to come with you. As far as I can."

"That would be to the Temple Mount. The plaza surrounding the Dome," explained Clooney. "From the plaza you can see everything. You can watch me enter the Dome, and you can watch me exit. Will that make you feel better?"

She nodded.

"Still, your idea of a disguise is not a bad idea," said Clooney. "Even in the plaza, the less attention you draw to yourself, the better."

"What do you suggest?"

"At the very least, a veil. Something to cover your head. If they see your blonde hair and green eyes, the Waqf may pull you aside for questioning. But whatever you do, just make sure you go nowhere near the Dome of the Rock. Don't even hint at it. Do you agree?"

She agreed.

In a nearby marketplace, Clooney directed Hannah through the vendors' stalls. He took her to the place his aunties shopped, and he haggled loudly with a shopkeeper, and once a price was agreed upon, he rifled through the stacks of clothing.

"What about this?" asked Hannah, holding up a blue dress and veil.

"No, try this one," insisted Clooney. "You look better in green. Green is definitely your colour."

Hannah tried the clothes on before a mirror in the back of the stall. In the end, they left with the dress, veil, and a pair of matching sandals as her disguise.

"How do I look?" she said, pulling the veil close about her cheek.

"Like a sad, pretty French girl, trying to dress like an Arab."

"How many times must I tell you. I am not French, I am from—"

"No, don't say it," he said, placing a finger to his lips. "You are from *Jerusalem*."

Hannah smiled, nodding. "Right, I am from Jerusalem..."

They wound their way through the Muslim Quarter, heading for the hill that led to the Temple Mount. In the distance, Hannah could already see the gold dome they were headed for.

"So you are saying," said Clooney, "you think Professor Weisman is the Grand Chancellor of the Cancellarii? And she is behind your grandfather's kidnapping?"

"She did pull a gun on me. And she admitted she has Henri."

"Then what about Andrepont? Where does he fit in?"

"That part is more confusing," she confessed. "Maybe there was a feud between them. Andrepont versus Professor Weisman. A fight for power within the Cancellarii. I do not know, and I do not care. I plan to keep my distance from them both."

Their path to the Temple Mount was through a narrow lane that doubled as a market. Along the way they passed several incense shops, bread shops, shops selling exquisitely fashioned lamps and antique frames. Clooney directed her left, into a long, dark alley, completely roofed over. It was almost like a tunnel, with more vendors and cafés lining the walls on either side. At the end of the long tunnel was a sunburst of light. It was so bright, Hannah could not see what lay beyond.

As they approached the tunnel's end and her eyes adjusted to the daylight, they climbed a set of broad stone steps. They halted atop the first landing, and she turned a circle in wonder.

"So this is the Temple Mount," she said. "I have always wondered what it looked like."

"This is just the beginning. There is another set of steps," said Clooney.

They climbed the second flight of stairs, and Hannah stopped in her tracks. There it was. The Dome of the Rock. She had no idea it would be so beautiful. The gigantic shrine rose from the centre of the plaza. It was octagon-shaped, with dazzling blue tiles and a huge golden dome above. Somewhere within the shrine lay a rock that was so sacred to the Muslims, they allowed no non-Muslims to enter.

Hannah glanced around. There were lots of people in the plaza. Most everyone was Muslim—the men wore beards, and some even wore turbans, while the women were covered in hijabs or burkas. Hopefully no one would pay her any mind. She sat down on a bench at the edge of the plaza and within view of the Dome of the Rock.

She took Clooney's hand. "You can do this."

He hung the camera about his neck and lifted the journal in assurance. "What could go wrong?"

Clooney waved goodbye to Hannah and started across the plaza. He wove his way through the crowds. Ahead, he saw the entry arch to the Dome of the Rock, and the two giant wooden doors stood open with guards posted on either side.

At the entrance, Clooney removed his shoes. The guards barely glanced at him as he passed through the doors and into the ancient shrine, and then he stopped.

Because it was amazing. It did not matter how many times he had visited, the inside of the Dome of the Rock was as breathtaking as ever. Sunlight entered through stained-glass windows. The floor was plush carpet, and the dome soared high above. Pillars formed a ring around the outer edge of the chamber. And in the very centre was the rock. It was huge. Like a giant, rough-hewn platform. As a Muslim, Clooney was taught to believe this was the exact spot their prophet Muhammad left earth for the heavenly realms. According to Hannah, it was also the place Jews believed Abraham prepared to offer his son to God. And Christians believed this was the very place Jesus was first presented to the temple. All three religions revered this location.

Glancing about, Clooney saw people kneeling in prayer. Careful not to disturb them, he quietly opened the journal. He found the illustration that included the rock before him. After a little repositioning, moving a little to the right and then back a full step, he found his view matched that of the journal's illustration.

"Perfect," he whispered to himself.

Now for the fun part.

He turned on the camera, just as Hannah had shown him. Peering through the viewfinder, he saw that the exposure settings were visible along the bottom:

$$f.8 \quad 80 \quad 600$$

Hannah had done her part correctly—for these were the same numbers Henri had written beneath the illustration.

With everything in place, Clooney snapped the photo and he was done. Easy.

He was looking at the buttons on the back of the camera, trying to figure out which button would allow him to review the photo he'd just taken, when someone tapped his shoulder.

Clooney turned around, and his heart jumped into his throat.

There they were, staring right back at him. Clooney tried to speak, but no words escaped his mouth.

"Thought you could get away?" said the biggest of the four boys.

Clooney's only thought was to run.

Hannah sat on the bench in the plaza, worrying, observing the people entering and exiting the Dome. Clooney had only just gone in and already her heart was drumming with impatience. How long would it take Clooney to locate the proper angle? And what if he couldn't? And what if he accidentally changed the camera's settings?

So many things could go wrong, and yet there was nothing she could do. Hannah had to let go. Just relax she told herself. Clooney knows what he's doing.

Just then, she noticed four young men strolling across the plaza. There was no mistaking them. It was the same four thugs Clooney claimed to have swindled—the same ones they had run from in the alleys and only barely escaped.

"Oh no!" she whispered aloud, standing up in alarm, her fingernails biting into her palms. She watched the young men remove their shoes before the shrine. They went in.

Hannah panicked. She had to warn Clooney. But what could she do? With no time for a plan, Hannah pulled the veil tight about her head till only her eyes could be seen and raced for the shrine.

When she reached the doors, she kicked off her sandals and kept her head low, avoiding the eyes of the guards and swept past them and into the Dome.

I'm inside, she thought. Even Professor Weisman had never made it this far. She was inside the Dome of the Rock, and it was beautiful, and no one had prevented her entry, and then she saw Clooney standing before all four thugs. She couldn't hear what was said, but Clooney raised a hand, as if to calm them. He took a step back. She saw one of the thugs snatch the journal from Clooney's hand and she cried out—she actually cried out. With no other thought than to get the journal back, Hannah thrust herself between Clooney and the thugs and grabbed the journal with both hands.

"That's mine!" she hissed, yanking back on the book.

"Hannah! Quiet!" whispered Clooney. "Everyone is looking!"

"Not! Until! I get! My journal back!"

She yanked harder, and then all at once the young man let go and Hannah fell back on her rear. The thugs turned tail and sprinted out the doors, leaving Hannah on the floor with her journal.

Clooney looked at her with horror and amazement.

"I got it," she breathed, standing up and brushing herself off. "I got the journal."

"But your hair!" he gasped.

Hannah lifted a hand to her head and immediately knew what was wrong. Her veil had fallen back when she hit the floor. Now she stood in the center of the shrine, journal in hand, her head completely exposed with her blonde hair shining for all to see.

She quickly pulled the veil over her head but it was too late. With all the commotion, everyone was already watching. Everyone had seen. Before she could even slip the journal into her backpack, a Waqf guard had her and Clooney each in his grip.

"You will come with me," he said in a voice so calm and emotionless, Hannah knew not to test him. Without another word, the guard marched them out the tall double doors and toward a fate Hannah dare not imagine.

Inside the small administration building of the Waqf author-ities, located just off the Temple Mount plaza, Hannah and Clooney sat in white plastic chairs in an office. The office was baking hot. A tired fan huffed warm air about the walls, turn-ing left, then right, then left again, lifting puffs of paper upon the desk with each rotation.

The official on the other side of the desk was an older man, Palestinian, wearing a dark suit and glasses. If his hair was shaved any shorter he would be bald. His eyebrow was more like a mustache on his forehead, having grown into one bushy mass. He had a strong, sharp nose and impatient dark eyes. On the whole, it was a humourless face that said Iqbal Hazdeen, the owner of this desk, took his job very, very seriously.

"Are we under arrest?" asked Hannah.

Mr. Hazdeen sorted through the papers on his desk. He began writing in a file. Without looking up, he said, "Not yet, but you will be shortly. We have contacted the police, and they will be here soon."

Hannah couldn't believe she was being arrested. She wasn't a bad child. Would she go to jail? And what about Clooney, would he go to jail too?

"This is my fault," she said. "Please let Clooney go."

"Clooney?" the man gave her a puzzled look. "You mean this boy? Samir Yusef?"

She nodded, and Mr. Hazdeen returned to his files, writ-ing furiously. He said, "Samir Yusef was your guide. Your accomplice. As a Muslim, Samir knows better than to assist a non-Muslim into the shrine. He is as guilty as you."

Mr. Hazdeen closed the first file and opened a second one. He turned to Hannah.

"Your name?" he said.

She told him, and Mr. Hazdeen wrote it down in the file.

"And your father, where is he?"

"Dead."

"Your mother then. Where is your mother?"

"Brussels."

"Brussels?"

"Belgium. In Europe. My mother is in Europe."

"Who is looking after you?"

"No one."

Mr. Hazdeen gaped at her as though she were an alien. "You are alone?" he said. "How are you here, alone in Jerusalem?"

Hannah looked down, saying nothing.

She could feel Mr. Hazdeen staring at her, waiting for her answer. Finally he closed the file. "Very well. You do not need to answer me, as I have no jurisdiction within Israeli law. But when the police arrive you will be properly arrested. And when they ask you questions, I suggest you give answers."

Hannah shared a look with Clooney. They didn't need to speak. Each knew what the other was thinking.

Police meant Andrepont. Andrepont meant Cancellarii.

They were doomed.

There was a knock on Mr. Hazdeen's office door. "Yes?" he called.

An assistant poked his head in. He announced an Israeli police officer had arrived. Mr. Hazdeen gave Hannah a look of cold venom and exited the office. Out in the hall, she could hear him speaking with the officer. Mr. Hazdeen was explaining that Hannah had, as a non-Muslim, snuck into the Dome of the Rock. A grave offence. And Clooney had been her guide, which was nearly as bad. He demanded the police officer arrest them both immediately.

In response, the officer explained that it was an unfortunate situation. He wished Hannah and Clooney had been more respectful of Islamic custom and the guidelines set out by the Waqf. But the truth was, the police officer continued, no Israeli law had been broken. There was nothing he could do.

"Nothing you can do? But this is a absurd!" raged Mr. Hazdeen.

"I am sorry," the officer replied. "I understand your viewpoint, but it's simply not a police matter unless a state law has been broken."

Hannah couldn't believe her luck. They were actually going to walk free!

After a moment, the officer offered a suggestion. "Mr. Hazdeen, if you like, I can have a talk with the children," he said. "I can give them a bit of scare, so they understand the seriousness of the matter. Perhaps keep them from trying something like this again."

Hannah heard Mr. Hazdeen grumble in agreement and then the door to the office opened. The police officer stepped in and took one look at Hannah and then paused, looking at her, and Hannah knew in that instant that everything was not all right. She would not be walking free. From the look in the officer's eye, she knew he recognized her.

He's seen my picture, she thought. *He knows exactly who I am.*

If she had any doubts, they were wiped away in that moment, for the officer said, "Would you happen to be Hannah Dubuisson, by chance? The granddaughter of Henri Dubuisson?"

Hannah felt her stomach rise into her throat. She nodded.

Keeping his eyes glued on Hannah, he called the station on his radio. When dispatch responded, he said. "Remember that girl we're looking for? The Dubuisson child? Well, you can tell the inspector we found her. That's right. I have her now. Tell Andrepont we're on our way."

Hannah sat in the back of the police car. The officer hadn't handcuffed her, which she was eternally grateful for. He hadn't turned his siren on either. As they drove through the downtown district of modern Jerusalem, all she could think was, I can't believe I'm arrested. I can't believe I'm arrested.

Clooney was set free. Apparently Andrepont had no interest in him because the officer simply told Clooney to clear out. To be a good kid and not cause any more trouble with the Waqf. Before Clooney had left, he made hand signals to

Hannah, showing he would head to the police station and try to meet up with her there.

"I have information," Hannah told the officer in the front seat. He glanced in the rearview mirror, but said nothing. "I have information about some very dangerous criminals, right here in Jerusalem. One of them is a professor at the university."

"Save it for the inspector," the officer said.

Hannah was petrified with fear. Her hands trembled. She couldn't steady her breath. She was going to jail. She was actually going to jail. And if she were in jail, no one would rescue Henri. The Cancellarii would keep him hostage forever, or worse... get rid of him.

Hannah had tried so hard to make everything right, but everything was going wrong. Terribly wrong.

They pulled into the station's parking lot. The officer opened the rear door and guided Hannah out, but kept a hand on her shoulder as he led her through the station doors, passed the front desk, nodding at the uniformed receptionist, and headed straight down the hall.

Hannah recalled scenes from movies. *The interrogation room*. She imagined a dark, empty cell with a single chair and a bright light shining in the prisoner's eyes. A mean, angry policeman asking question after question until the prisoner gave in and finally told him everything he wanted to know.

But this station hall only had offices with glass doors and windows. Hannah peered within and saw people in suits, talking on phones, doing paperwork, with no sign of the terrifying interrogation rooms from her imagination.

The door at the end of the hall was open, and the officer led Hannah through. And there he was, Inspector Andrepont, sitting at his desk. Waiting for her.

As soon as she entered, Andrepont rose to greet her. "Please, sit," he said, indicating the couch against the wall. He almost seemed excited to see her.

Inspector Andrepont dismissed the officer who had led her in and then gave Hannah a genuine smile. "Mademoiselle Dubuisson," he said. "I am so glad you are safe. We have much to discuss. But before we begin, I must apologize."

An apology? This was not what Hannah had expected. She was speechless.

"When I first encountered you at your grandfather's home, I did not intend to frighten you. Though in looking back, I believe that is precisely what happened. I am told I sometimes have that effect. It is the frown, I believe. An unfortunate family trait." He smiled ruefully. "Nevertheless, it was my intention to help you. It was my promise, in fact. I have promised to help you."

"Promised who?" asked Hannah, still on her guard.

"Your grandfather, of course. The esteemed Henri Dubuisson."

"My grandfather? You know Henri Dubuisson?"

"We are excellent friends," he explained. "Henri and I go way back. All the way back to Brussels actually. We immigrated to Israel at the same time."

"But… how…" Hannah didn't even know what to ask next.

"I fear, Mademoiselle Dubuisson, you have had a rough arrival. On top of your grandfather's kidnapping, you have been chased left, right, and centre, and have no doubt had unfavourable dealings with his old enemy. The Cancellarii. For years they have been tracking him, hoping to discover your ancestor's ancient secret. Henri first came to me years ago, when he sought to uncover their plot. Since then, we have worked together in attempts to identify the Grand Chancellor and expose their secret society."

"But… the journal. When you came to Henri's apartment, you were looking for his journal."

"But of course! That crazy journal is Henri's life! The only thing he loves more than that journal is you, Mademoiselle. He made me promise to look after both if trouble arose. And clearly it has. Henri became quite suspicious about a week before your arrival. He warned me the Cancellarii might make their move. He said he was being followed."

"By Professor Weisman!" she said. "Is that why you were at the university?"

"Indeed. Once I realized Weisman was the Grand Chancellor, I went to make the arrest. It was quite a coincidence to discover you at the same time."

"Did you get her? Is she arrested?"

"I'm afraid not," he replied. "Weisman managed to escape. Which means she and her Cancellarii are still out there. They will be looking for you, Mademoiselle, and the journal you carry." He looked at her now, and she saw genuine concern in his eyes. "I must say, it is an immense relief to see you safe. I feared I had broken my promise to Henri and lost both you and the journal to the Cancellarii. And if you must know the truth, I did not look forward to Henri's response." He grinned. "He can be quite…"

"*Passionate*," said Hannah. "He is passionate."

"Thank you, a perfect description. Our Henri is passionate. And does not hesitate to speak his mind."

"So what now? How will you get Henri back? And capture Weisman and the Cancellarii?"

He grimaced. "We are working on that."

"You don't know," she said. "You don't know where Henri is."

"But we will," Inspector Andrepont assured her. "We still have a few leads. The important thing is that you are safe now. And I am here to help you. But where are you going? Please, sit down!"

"I know how to get Henri back," she said, standing to leave. "And I cannot do it from here. I cannot explain any more. I must finish what I have started."

"Mademoiselle, even if I had not promised to look after you, I could not let you go free. This is now a police matter. You are in grave danger and are furthermore a child. I cannot allow you to wander the streets."

"Inspector Andrepont," she began. "Who first discovered the identity of the Cancellarii's Grand Chancellor? You or I?"

"Well, that would be… you, mademoiselle. I believe you happened upon that information first."

"Correct. And who," continued Hannah, "has managed to stay one step ahead of the Cancellarii? And the police force, too, I might add?"

"I confess, you have done very well for a child. All things considered."

"And who was entrusted with this journal? And knows how to read it? And therefore has the clues needed to find the treasure, and so Henri as well?"

Inspector Andrepont appeared distinctly unhappy. "You," he said.

"And who," said Hannah, "is the only person with an actual plan for getting Henri back?"

Inspector Andrepont stared at Hannah, his fingers drumming the edge of his desk.

"You have made your point."

"Admit it, Inspector. I am your best chance of finding Henri. Keeping me here is to no one's advantage."

Andrepont studied her and then shook his head in defeat. "I should have known Henri's granddaughter would be stubborn as an ox. You have his eyes, do you know that?"

She said nothing. A far off voice in her mind whispered, *you have the magic eye...*

"Henri has the strongest disposition of any man I've known," he continued. "A good friend to have. But not an easy one. Something tells me you aren't going to give up on this, are you?"

Hannah held his gaze. "Are you going to stop me?"

He sighed, opening his hands in a gesture of helplessness. "I am an officer of the law. My hands are tied. If I gave a child permission to leave this station, with no supervision, I would lose my job in a heartbeat."

He paused, giving her a significant look. "However," he said. "I must now make a photocopy of your file. The photocopier is all the way down the hall. It is a long walk. And while at the photocopier, I may stop to chat with a friend or two. I may even get a cup of coffee. It could take me ten, perhaps even fifteen minutes before I return…"

He continued looking at her, making sure Hannah understood. Then Inspector Andrepont grabbed the file and stood.

He nodded meaningfully and headed out the door.

Hannah couldn't believe it. Andrepont was letting her go. Technically, she would be escaping, still running from the law, but she knew Andrepont wouldn't stop her. She took two business cards from his desk. One card she placed in her backpack. On the second card, she wrote:

Thank you…

She left the message on the inspector's desk, exited the office, walked briskly down the hall and out the front door as if she had been sauntering out of police stations all her life.

Standing on the pavement out front, with a look of joy and relief, was Clooney. Faithful as ever.

Hannah had never been happier to see a pair of ridiculously ill-fitting sunglasses.

On the bus back to the Old City of Jerusalem, Hannah filled Clooney in on Andrepont and his actual friendship with Henri. It seemed that nothing was the way she first assumed. The treasure of King Solomon's temple turned out to be a magical ring of wisdom. Henri's friend from the university was actually his worst enemy. And the man Hannah feared most was now suddenly her ally. What else could possibly be turned on its head?

Well, the next illustration, of course...

Hannah opened the journal to the sixth illustration. Flipping it right side up, she studied it, trying to get a sense of where it might be. It appeared to be the upper part of a small arch. The arch was carved, and the area around it was adorned with candles and tapestries. Without clues to guide her, it was impossible to say exactly where it might be, so she removed her camera and switched on the power.

Hannah pressed the button to review the last photograph. It was the one Clooney took at the Dome of the Rock before her arrest.

In the picture, she saw the rock itself where Muhammad, the prophet of Islam, supposedly departed for heaven. Superimposed upon the rock, Hannah saw the ghostly image of a cross. But not just any cross. Each of the cross's four arms were equal in size. And surrounding the cross were four more crosses, exactly the same, only smaller.

Clooney sighed. "I'm Muslim. You are Jewish. Too bad we don't have a third person along, someone who actually knows something about Christianity and crosses."

"Funny you should say that," said Hannah, clutching the medallion around her neck and lifting it for him to see. "We would never have figured it out, if it were not for this."

"It's the same cross!" exclaimed Clooney. "Do you know what it means?"

"Henri said this cross is called the 'Order of the Holy Sepulcher'. It was the symbol used by Jerusalem's knights long ago. Their job was to protect the Holy Sepulcher itself."

"The Holy Sepulcher? What's that?"

"I will show you."

"You mean you know where it is?"

"Of course. It is the most famous Christian church in the world. And it's easy to find. We just follow the Via Dolorosa."

Hannah and Clooney departed the bus, entering the Old City through Jaffa Gate. Once inside, they found themselves in the Christian Quarter of Jerusalem and walking along a cobbled lane known at the Via Dolorosa, which meant, 'Way of Suffering'. It was the supposed path Jesus had walked while carrying the cross. Along the Via they passed countless shops selling crosses, antiques, cheap souvenirs, T-shirts, framed images of Jesus, and many sellers of books. Instead of orthodox Jews with their black brimmed hats, or women in hijabs buying vegetables in the Arab market, the streets of the Christian Quarter were swarming with nuns in their blue habits and priests in long gowns. It was like another world entirely.

There were also many tour groups, with tour guides pointing out the various stations along the path that Jesus supposedly walked toward his crucifixion.

And all the tours led to the same place. The Church of the Holy Sepulcher. In the church's outer court, tour groups congregated in a seething mass, waiting their turn for entry. According to Christians, this was the place Jesus was crucified on the cross. It also held the tomb where Jesus' body was interred, or laid to rest.

As Hannah looked up at the imposing front wall, feeling the excitement of those people waiting to get in, she couldn't help but see a pattern emerging.

Jesus was a direct descendant of King Solomon. For Christians, this church was their holiest site. Just like the Dome of the Rock for the Muslims. And the Western Wall for the Jews.

The map in Hannah's backpack appeared to be taking her on a tour through the last three-thousand years of Israel's major religions—from Judaism, to Islam, and lastly to Christianity—all of them locked together by a shared history in this solitary, enchanted city and a magical ring once worn by its wisest king.

Hannah and Clooney entered the church. The first thing they saw were several people crowded around a flat, rectangular stone on the floor. The people kneeled or crouched and rubbed the flat stone with black plastic bags. Hannah sensed this wasn't what she was looking for, but couldn't help wondering what was going on. She asked a nun beside her.

The nun was Filipino and answered in broken English that this was called the 'the stone of anointing.' It was believed to be the stone Jesus' body was laid upon after his death. The black plastic bags, the nun explained with a smile, were filled with souvenirs and cheap trinkets people had purchased in the markets, which they hoped to bless by rubbing them against the stone.

The nun attached herself to Hannah and Clooney as their guide, clearly inspired to share what she felt were the most significant parts of this church.

Moving on, Hannah was shown room after room with high vaulted ceilings and wonderfully carved walls and colorful lanterns and candles and much goldwork on altars. It was a feast for the eyes. But it wasn't until the nun led them into the rotunda that Hannah knew, with complete certainty, she had found what she sought.

The rotunda was a large chamber with a domed ceiling high above. In the center of the dome was a round opening that let in the sun, and it beamed down upon them, lighting the entirety of the chamber.

And there in the center of the chamber stood the crypt of Jesus.

The crypt was like a small stone temple in itself, situated in the center of the room. A long line of people wound around the crypt, waiting for their turn to enter and pray before Jesus' tomb.

But what interested Hannah was not the crypt, or the long queues of people, or the spectacular sunlight beaming down from above. It was the arch. The little arch leading into the tomb. It was identical to the sixth illustration in her journal.

Hannah thanked their guide and politely sent her away.

"That's the place," whispered Clooney, pointing to the decorative arch above the tomb's doorway.

Hannah nodded, removing her camera from her backpack. She adjusted the camera settings so they matched the encoded exposure in the journal:

$$f.1.4 \quad 160 \quad 2600$$

She snapped the photo.

She pushed the button to review the picture.

"Whoa…" said Clooney. "Are those what I think they are?"

Hannah could only stare.

This image was *not* like the others.

The camera in Hannah's hands displayed an image of the arch above Jesus' tomb. The actual arch and the image were identical. But unlike the actual arch, the camera's version included a second image on top of it. The second image looked like the phantom of a ruined wall, standing alone in the sea, completely surrounded by water. And below the wall were written a series of symbols:

"They look like hieroglyphs," said Clooney.

"They are," said Hannah. "They're Egyptian."

"How do you know for certain?"

"Because I can read them. Henri taught me."

Clooney looked dumbstruck. Apparently most children here in Jerusalem weren't taught Egyptian hieroglyphics along with their ABCs. But then, most children didn't have Henri Dubuisson for a grandfather.

She quickly translated the glyphs into this:

A C R E

That was the easy part. It was the wall that stumped her. The strange ruined wall, surrounded by water. Who had ever heard of an ancient wall in the ocean? And how did it get there? It was magnificent and magical, but part of Hannah wondered if the wall really existed.

"Well," she said. "I have no idea where the wall is. But I can read the glyphs. They spell ACRE."

"What's ACRE?" asked Clooney.

"I don't know."

"And why would Julien write in Egyptian?"

Hannah thought about it. "That part makes sense, actually. Israel was once part of Egypt. Right up until about 2000 BCE. Maybe he is directing us toward something very old."

"What in Israel could be *that* old?"

Hannah didn't know. She decided to give the Internet a shot. As she typed ACRE into the search bar, she wondered what Henri would think if he realized just how much of her 'archaeological sleuthing' had been accomplished by Google.

The Internet brought back over two-hundred-million pages related to the search word: ACRE.

Hannah quickly glanced through the first five hits. Each one described an *acre* as a British unit of measurement. A measurement of land. Somehow Hannah didn't think this definition fit.

"Let's sit down," she said. "I need to think."

"Sounds good to me. I need a coffee."

They left the church of the Holy Sepulcher and took seats at an outdoor café in the Christian Quarter. Hannah ordered fresh squeezed orange juice and a falafel. Clooney had his coffee, and then another. They watched the people from every corner of the world, in every mode of dress, wandering the narrow lanes.

As Hannah observed a cat hunting scraps beneath the tables, her mind ran through possibilities, trying to figure out what *acre* meant. What was Julien trying to tell her with this clue? There was only one illustration left. She felt certain that once she understood the meaning of acre, she would reach the last point on the map and therefore the Seal of Solomon.

"*Acre, acre, acre...*" she whispered to herself, pronouncing it differently each time, hoping the sound itself might jolt some realization. "*Acre, acre, acre...*"

"Did you say Akko?" asked Clooney, looking at his reflection in the sheen of the granite table. He had spent the last few minutes searching for the first signs of a moustache.

Hannah looked at him. "No."

He continued to turn his head this way and that to better view his top lip. "Oh. For a minute, I thought you said Akko."

"I don't even know what that is. What is Akko?"

"Just a place," he said. "Some place my uncle took us one summer. A port town up north on the Haifa Bay."

"Akko is a place?"

"That's how we say it in Arabic, anyway. I don't know what you would call it in French. Will you look at this for me? Right here… I think this might be a hair."

Hannah ignored him, feeling the spark of an idea.

Out came the phone and good old Google. This time, instead of searching for *acre*, she did an Internet search for Akko.

Immediately, her phone filled with hit after hit, page after page, all of them about a famous UNESCO heritage city in the north. The city of Akko, the Internet said, was one of the *oldest continuously inhabited cities in the world*. So far, a perfect fit. They needed something old, and Akko was that.

She read on. About midway down the page she halted, her eyes glued to the phone.

"Clooney," she said, barely able to contain her excitement. "Read what this says."

She passed him the phone. He began scanning the article, his lips mumbling as he read. Then his eyes bugged out and he turned to her. "It says Akko is the new name for the city. The original name was *Acre*."

"This is it!" she cried. "*Acre* is what Akko was called in Julien's day. That's where the wall in the sea is located!"

"And somewhere inside that wall," said Clooney, "will be the Seal of Solomon…"

The sun was setting. All across the city, the domes and towers and ancient stone walls of Jerusalem took on a ruddy hue. In the mosques, loudspeakers crackled to life, and the haunting voices of the muezzin singers called Muslims to pray.

"We should take the train," said Clooney. "There's a night train that goes all the way to Akko. We will be there by morning."

Hannah wanted to take a cab to the railway station, but her emergency fund was running low, and she had no idea how much two tickets to Akko would cost. So they walked.

It was a long walk, and the whole way, Hannah was on the look out for Cancellarii spies. She nearly jumped out of her skin each time a motorcycle sped by, or when someone's eyes lingered overlong or turned to follow her passing. It was night-time when they reached the railway station. It stood alone on the road, bathed in a halogen glow, the ticket booth and turn-stiles out front.

"Two tickets to Akko," said Hannah. She paid for their passage, and they squeezed through the turnstiles, awaiting the next train on the platform.

Waiting on the platform with them was a small group of backpackers. Teenagers sitting on huge rucksacks, texting on phones. There was also a family of orthodox Jews, three young Israeli soldiers in uniform, perhaps heading home on holiday, and a Palestinian woman with several children.

Hannah watched the children playing, the soldiers joking, the backpackers staring into the electronic glow of their phones.

"Can you believe we only met two days ago?" she said to Clooney. "It seems like so much has happened. A whole lifetime even."

"I know. It is hard to believe. And you still haven't even kissed me."

She smirked. "And you keep saying I am sad and lonely. Even though I have never been happier."

"Happy? Even with your grandfather missing?"

"I'm frightened for him, yes. Not a moment goes by I am not thinking of him or what I must do to get Henri back. But I'm more excited than I can ever remember. I guess I enjoy adventure and know Henri would understand." She thought for a moment. "And though I cannot explain it, I have this feeling everything will turn out. It is almost like Julien Dubuisson is watching over our shoulder, smiling, because everything is going according to plan."

"You think there is a plan?"

"His plan. Julien's plan. After all, we are following in the footsteps of a *sorcier*."

A loudspeaker announced the train's arrival in two minutes and the backpackers stood and stretched and shouldered their rucksacks. The Palestinian woman rounded up her children.

The train cruised in to a smooth halt at the platform and the doors slid open. "Here we go," said Hannah.

Their train car was nearly empty. Just the backpackers at the front end, Hannah and Clooney at the back. All the seats in the middle were empty. The doors slid shut, the train rolled out from the platform and they were off to Akko. The last point on the map. By this time tomorrow, Hannah might have the Seal of Solomon in her hand, ready to exchange it for Henri.

Hannah plugged her phone into the seat's charger and looked out the window. The night whipped by in its blackness, dotted with city lights. The stars and the moon slowly drifted in the sky. Hannah knew she should sleep, but she was too excited. Life was crackling before her eyes, and she was on a treasure hunt, a genuine adventure, and it was all so much to take in. Her body refused to relax.

In the seat beside her, Clooney asked, "Have you ever wondered how your grandfather figured all this out? I mean, the encoded exposures? Deciphering the map?"

"Constantly."

"Do you think it was just luck? Maybe he accidentally entered the right numbers into the camera and suddenly... poof! The enchanted image appears, and he's cracked the code!"

"No," Hannah shook her head. "It couldn't work like that. There are just too many possible combinations. Too many settings on the camera. Luck could not explain it. He did something else."

"Like what?"

She shook her head, still gazing out the window. "I would give just about anything to find out."

They arrived in Akko at dawn. Hannah woke as the train shuddered to a halt at the platform. She yawned and looked out the window and saw the sun rising over the city. Clooney had slept with his sunglasses on, his blue Aeropostale T-shirt spotted with drool. "We are here," she said.

"I know," he said, popping awake, acting as though he hadn't been snoring against her shoulder just moments before.

The train doors slid open. Hannah grabbed her backpack. She and Clooney stood to leave, and that's when she saw the man. He was Israeli, inconspicuous, nothing too interesting about his appearance. He was seated about midway down the car. He must have gotten on the train after she had fallen asleep. He wore sunglasses and gazed out the window, giving no sign of alarm. In his right ear was a radio bud.

Clooney nudged her. "Cancellarii?" he asked.

"Actually, I think it's police this time. Inspector Andrepont is probably keeping an eye on me, just to be safe."

"Do you want to give him the slip?"

She nodded.

"All right," said Clooney, rubbing his hands together. "Leave this one to me."

He led Hannah toward the open doors of the train. The officer secretly glanced their way and shifted in his seat, prepared to give chase as soon they exited. But before getting off, Clooney grabbed Hannah's arm.

"Wait," he said, loud enough for the undercover officer to hear. "Your backpack is open."

Hannah paused on the threshold, and Clooney pretended to fiddle with the zipper on her backpack. All the while, the seated officer grew anxious. He clearly wanted to keep track of them, but didn't want to stand up yet and announce his intentions.

The train's intercom chimed. A recorded message announced, "Please step back from the doors. The train is departing in ten seconds."

The man fidgeted at the edge of his seat, watching Hannah like a hawk.

"*Wait*," whispered Clooney, holding Hannah in place by her backpack.

The intercom chimed again. "Please step back from the door. The train is departing in—"

"Wait…" Clooney hissed.

The doors rattled in their tracks and began to shut. The officer leapt from his seat, and Clooney shoved Hannah out the doors and onto the station's platform, diving through after her. The doors shut tight, and the officer slammed up against them, stuck inside.

As the train rolled from the platform, Clooney waved at the officer on board. It was not a happy face that stared back at Hannah through the window of the departing train. She and Clooney stood on the platform, watching the train grow smaller and smaller.

"It's almost getting too easy," commented Clooney.

"We are basically professional outlaws at this point," she agreed, tapping her chin. "Who knew summer vacation could be so educational?"

Clooney turned to her. "So now what?"

"Internet," she said, removing her phone. She thumbed in 'Akko Wikipedia.'

"Let's see. The Wikipedia entry says Akko is an important harbour city and has been for thousands of years. Traders from all over the world used to gather here, exchanging exotic cargo at the ports. And listen to this… it says around 800 years ago, the crusaders built a *wall* around the entire city. The wall extended right out into the bay, protecting the harbours from invading fleets. But over time, the wall fell into ruin, and most of it was washed away." She read quietly to herself for a moment and then added aloud, "And here's what we are looking for… it says there are bits and pieces, little remnants of the wall still standing in the sea."

"That must be it. If we just walk along the harbours," suggested Clooney, "we can follow the outer edge of the city and keep our eyes open. I don't think either of us would miss anything as big as a wall rising up from the sea."

It was a good plan, and they started at once. It turned out most of the shoreline, where Akko met Haifa Bay, had been paved. Some of the paving was recent. And in some places, the seawater splashed up against huge chunks of stone, piled long ago to disrupt oncoming tides. Fishermen balanced upon the stones, casting lines into the sea. Boats of every size and colour bobbed just off shore.

"Look there," said Clooney, pointing out a great heap of stone blocks, perhaps fifty feet off shore, forming a mound above the surface of the water. The mound could have been part of a wall once, but was now tumbled into disarray.

They walked. Sometimes they hopped from stone block to stone block, chasing seagulls from their roosts. Just as the sun rose above the city, giving the bay a burnished glow, Hannah saw something in the distance. She stopped in her tracks, shielding the glare from her eyes. "Is that…?"

She and Clooney stared for a moment. Without a word, he grabbed her hand and they raced along the harbour, only halting when they reached the harbour's overlook. There, rising from the sea like a bizarre island of stacked stones, was the remnant of a long ago wall. The Crusader Wall. It looked for all the world like something from a dream, standing alone at sea, the tide washing about the great slabs of its footing.

The Crusader Wall stood two stories tall. There was even a window in the wall, which was probably a cannon-slot at one time, used to protect the bay from enemy ships. And as the sunlight entered through the far side of the window and the sea crashed about and slapped the stones with a gentle boom, Hannah felt she had stepped into the pages of some fantastical storybook.

"The last point on the map," said Clooney at her side. "You found it, Hannah. You actually found it."

She turned to him. "*We* found it," she said. "We found it together."

Clooney beamed. He may have worn silly sunglasses instead of armour and preferred dancing to jousts, but

Hannah felt she couldn't have chosen a better knight to accompany her on this modern-day fable.

Clooney said, "Let's take a look at that last illustration."

Hannah opened the journal and they looked at it together. The seventh and last illustration showed the lone wall, surrounded by seawater, and it appeared to be drawn from this very viewpoint on the harbour.

Hannah aligned the compositions till the camera matched the illustration. She glanced back in the journal to get the code, the three numbers Henri had deciphered, and then her heart dropped, staring in disbelief.

There were no numbers beneath the illustration.

Panicked, Hannah flipped the page, but there was nothing more to see. The rest of the journal was blank. In her excitement to reach their destination, Hannah had never noticed the missing code.

"I don't understand," said Clooney. "What does it mean?"

"It means Henri never made it this far. He did not finish deciphering the map."

"But what do we do? This is terrible!"

Without the proper settings, Hannah knew the camera wouldn't decode the illustration. Which meant no Seal of Solomon. Which meant no freeing Henri from the Cancellarii. To fail at this point, she thought, was simply unacceptable.

There had to be a way.

She returned to the front of the journal. There on the first page, she saw the blue post-it note Henri had first sent her. He had given her three instructions.

1. Keep the map safe

Hannah had done that. And she had done a fine job, considering all she was up against.

2. Beware the *Cancellarii*

Hannah had succeeded there too, or at least she had done her best. Henri would have been proud if he knew how cleverly she had evaded his old enemy.

3. Remember, Hannah, you have the magic eye!

This one was a little different. Hannah had her camera, true, and it had solved much of the mystery. But all along, Hannah had wondered if there might be something more to her grandfather's third and final message.

You have the magic eye…

Hannah found herself considering all she had seen in her last three days of adventuring through Israel, all she been through in order to reach this very site. She was slowly coming to appreciate a logic, what could even be called a *plan*, woven like a melody throughout each of the seven locations Julien Dubuisson had led her to.

With the creation of his enchanted map, Julien had ensured no seeker of wisdom could access the *Khātim Sulaymāni*, the Seal of Solomon, until they had travelled his course and seen everything he intended them to see, including the three major sites of Judaism, Christianity, and Islam.

Now, having seen them herself, how could Hannah possibly set one place of worship above the other, when each was equally magnificent? She had seen the same thing in the eyes of each person, no matter which place of worship they prayed at. We all wanted the same things. We were all human. Deep down, there really was very little difference between us.

This, Hannah realized, was Julien's way of ensuring King Solomon's safeguard remained in place. Only with wisdom could one access the hidden wisdom of the ring.

And as Hannah marvelled at this realization and the brilliance of Julien's grand design, something opened in her heart. With spectacular clarity, she saw in her mind's eye the hand of her grandfather as he wrote the blue post-it note. As though moving backward in time at incredible speed, she next saw her grandfather strolling through Jerusalem, the journal cradled in his arm. Henri kneeling before the Western Wall, deciphering the first illustration. Henri at her father's funeral. The images kept rolling backward. Next, Henri as a child, receiving the journal from his own father, and on down the line, generation after generation, until Hannah could see in her own mind the detailed image of her great ancestor, Julien Dubuisson himself, sorcerer of Napoleon's court, sketching out the seven illustrations, adding just a touch of enchantment, which ultimately led to this place, where Hannah now stood.

Hannah experienced the ghostly apparition of Julien Dubuisson, standing in the exact spot she stood now; no longer separated by time, he gazed upon the lonely wall in the sea, his hand like a visor at his brow, just as hers was now.

Three numbers. Hannah saw three numbers in her mind. Burning like wheels of fire.

It was the code.

She finally knew how Henri had done it. Like him, and all her grandfathers before her, Hannah Dubuisson had the magic eye.

In the journal of Julien Dubuisson, just beneath the seventh illustration of a ruined crusader wall standing alone in the sea, Hannah wrote three numbers.

f.11   250   200

"You… deciphered the illustration?" asked Clooney in wonder.

"I guess it runs in the family."

"Runs in the family? The only thing that runs in our family is baldness, a weakness for sweets, and a love of good jokes. How did you luck out with magic powers?"

She shrugged, digging out the camera. Using the three numbers she had seen in her mind, she set the encoded exposure. She snapped the photo of the Crusader Wall and looked at it.

In the photo, she saw the Crusader Wall with the sunlight pouring through the cannon-slot. Superimposed atop the cannon-slot was the ghostly image of a six-pointed star. The symbol of the *Khātim Sulaymāni*. The Seal of Solomon.

"That's it," she said, pointing to the star. "Inside the window is the treasure. King Solomon's legendary ring."

Hannah and Clooney climbed down the embankment that led to the sea. The tide was low and washed about their knees. They waded out to the Crusader Wall, which was not far from shore, and began to climb. The outer edge of the wall looked as though it had been unzipped from the rest, with the stones protruding from the side like handholds. The climb wasn't difficult, and they quickly reached the top. The wall was roughly three feet wide at the top, with plenty of room for them to move about.

They located the window, or cannon-slot, just below them. First Clooney, then Hannah, climbed over the edge and let themselves down the side of the wall until they reached the window.

The window was about five feet tall and four feet across—nearly the size of a small doorway, with space enough for both of them to stand. Hannah looked around. The interior of the space was built of stones, same as the rest of the wall. There were no obvious compartments. No secret doors that she could see. Hannah wasn't sure what to do next.

"Perhaps there is a loose stone?" said Clooney.

"Right, let's try."

Hannah removed her umbrella from her backpack and worked it between various stones in the wall, searching for a loose one. Clooney tested stones along the ceiling. Nodding at her umbrella, he said, "I admit, you get more use out of that umbrella than I expected."

She pried at a particularly large stone before her. She huffed and grunted. "Henri always said an umbrella is an archaeologist's second most important tool."

"What's the first?"

"Curiosity," she said, pausing to catch her breath. "Without it, there could be no wonder. No drive to discover. He used to say people could walk the same ground for a thousand years and think nothing of it. Until the archaeologist comes along, and with little more than the curiosity in her heart, reveals the truth beneath your very feet."

"Say that again…" said Clooney.

"The truth beneath your feet?" she repeated.

They froze, their eyes locked in realization. Hannah and Clooney crouched to inspect the stones at their feet.

"This one," cried Clooney, pointing to a stone darker than the rest. "This one is different. It must have been placed here later than the others!"

Hannah wedged her umbrella's tip down into the slot beside it, prying it back. When the corner lifted out, Clooney grabbed the stone with both hands and flipped it over.

There was a small hollow beneath the stone. In the hollow was an iron box, nearly orange with rust. Hannah picked the box up. The rust was so thick, she couldn't even see the lid's seam. She knocked the side, and flakes of rust rained down, revealing a small, corroded latch. She opened the latch and lifted the lid.

Inside the box was a ring.

It appeared to be made of iron and brass, just as the legend said. Four jewels, each colored red, yellow, green, and blue, were set into an imprint of the six-pointed star. And burned into the band itself were four symbols. Four letters.

The four letters of the secret name of God. The legend was true.

Hannah looked at Clooney and actually saw a tear on his cheek. He quickly swiped it away and said, "This is amazing, Hannah. I can't believe we actually found the Seal of Solomon. The legendary ring of wisdom."

Holding the ring, Hannah was reminded of the medallion around her neck, and what it had first felt like to find it. She had been wonderstruck. To think that a knight, nearly a thousand years prior, had carried that tiny cross and possibly worn it about his neck…

Now Hannah was looking upon the most wondrous artifact of all. King Solomon's ring. A treasure beyond treasures. And she was going to give it to the last person on earth who deserved it. The Grand Chancellor of the Cancellarii, Professor Weisman.

It was an archaeologist's worst nightmare, and she knew Henri would be horrified. When she considered that the ring may even have magical powers, the idea of handing it over to the Cancellarii was all the worse. Henri wouldn't just be horrified— he would forbid it. He would forbid the exchange of the ring for his own freedom, even if it cost his life.

"I don't think I can follow through with this," said Hannah, gazing at the ring in her palm.

"But you must. To get your grandfather back!"

She shook her head in confusion. "But I don't even think Henri would want me to. Julien Dubuisson did everything he could to keep this ring out of harm's way. Now I am about to hand-deliver it to his enemies."

Hannah began to cry. "I don't know what to do. What should I do, Clooney?"

He looked at her. "Drink coffee."

"What?" she said, a surprised chuckle rising up through the tears.

"It is always the answer," he said. "When in doubt, drink coffee. Look, you have your family traditions, passed down from one generation to the next. I have mine. My family makes coffee. We are coffee makers. My family is made of coffee. If I could open my veins and show you my blood—"

"I get it," said Hannah, sniffling. "And you are right. A fresh start makes sense. Where is the nearest café?"

Hannah slipped the ring into the front pocket of her dress, and they climbed back down the Crusader Wall. They waded out through the surf to the embankment and clambered up to the harbour. Cafés were everywhere.

"Take your pick," said Clooney.

They sat at a table overlooking the bay, the Crusader Wall still in plain view. Clooney ordered two coffees.

Hannah drank hers and sat back in her seat. "You were right. Coffee," she said. Her head was already clearing. The beginning of a plan was taking shape. She looked out over the water, tapping her chin. "I think I am going to call them."

"Who?" replied Clooney, spooning the coffee foam from the bottom of the cup. "Professor Weisman or Andrepont?"

"Both," she said. She removed her phone and dialed the first number.

"Wait! Shouldn't we think this through first?"

"I already have. Hello? This is Hannah Dubuisson speaking..."

The two phone calls were essentially the same. Hannah informed both Professor Weisman and Inspector Andrepont that she had what they wanted. For Weisman, that meant she had the Seal of Solomon. For Andrepont, that meant Henri, whom Professor Weisman was instructed to bring with her in order to complete the exchange.

"Meet me in Akko at five o'clock this evening," she told them. "I'll be standing on the harbour overlooking the Crusader Wall."

After finishing the phone calls, Hannah felt an unexpected flood of relief. It was done, and there was no going back. If all went well, Henri would be free by nightfall, and Andrepont would have his criminals in handcuffs. And Solomon's ring would likely go to a museum somewhere safe, where people could marvel at the wonders of human history.

Suddenly finding themselves with time on their hands, Hannah and Clooney wandered Akko for the remainder of the day. They strolled the Arab market and ate hummus so fresh it was served warm with pita bread. They toured the crusader castles and fed seagulls from the parapets.

When evening came, and the sun began to set, they headed back through the city to reach their rendezvous at the harbor. They waited beside a railing that overlooked the bay. In the twilight, the Crusader Wall glowed red, and a stiff wind blew Hannah's hair. The tide had come in, and now the sea beat at the embankment, sending salty spray across the pavement where they stood.

"Where is Andrepont?" asked Clooney, looking about. "Isn't he supposed to arrive first and arrest Professor Weisman when she gets here?"

"He will be hiding," she answered. "He is probably already watching us from someplace nearby. Waiting to spring on Weisman and her Cancellarii once Henri is out in the open."

"And here she comes, look," said Clooney. At that moment a familiar black sedan with tinted windows pulled up.

The driver got out, and Hannah recognized him. It was Jurowitz, the security guard from the university. Jurowitz opened the passenger front door and out stepped Professor Weisman. She wore a fancy blue dress and high-heel shoes, as though she were already celebrating what would soon be hers.

Professor Weisman left Jurowitz standing beside the car and approached Hannah and Clooney alone, following the railing. Even before she reached them, she addressed Hannah, saying, "My dear, Hannah. It appears Henri Dubuisson is no longer the sole archaeologist in your family. I always knew you were clever, but the Seal of the Solomon? King Solomon's own ring?" She paused before them with the hint of a smile. "Very impressive. All along I had expected it would be Henri who found the treasure and led me to it. But no matter. Let me see the ring."

"Where is Henri? You said you would bring Henri."

"First show me the ring."

Hannah shook her head. "No. I must see Henri first."

"Always the stubborn girl. One day that hard head of yours might land you in trouble. Just look what it's done for your grandfather." Weisman signaled to Jurowitz. He opened the rear door of the sedan and yanked Henri to his feet. Henri's white mustache was bushier than ever, and he appeared to have his hands tied behind his back. But even from this distance, Hannah could see his face was beaming.

"Henri!" she called. "Henri, are you all right?"

"I am fine, Hannah, just fine! And now that I see you, I am even better!"

Henri moved to greet her, and Jurowitz stopped him with a pistol, pressing it into Henri's side. Hannah gasped, and Clooney clutched her shoulder.

"Your reunion will have to wait," said Weisman. "First, we have a deal to complete. Let's start with the ring. If it truly is the Seal of Solomon, your grandfather will go free. But if this is a trick of some kind, things will not go well for you. Or your dear Henri. Do we understand each other?"

Hannah nodded. But inside she was churning. Where was Andrepont? The inspector should have arrived by now. If he didn't show up quickly, she would actually have to turn the ring over to Weisman to get Henri back.

Professor Weisman seemed to notice Hannah glancing about. "You are expecting someone?" she said, glancing around with Hannah. "Inspector Andrepont, perhaps?"

Hannah gasped. Weisman gave a smug grin and said, "Or perhaps your inspector is already here."

Weisman signaled Jurowitz again. He opened the car's other rear door, and this time dragged out Inspector Andrepont, placing him at gunpoint beside Henri.

"I am so sorry, Hannah," Andrepont called to her from the car. "They caught me from behind, just moments ago. You best do what they say, or I fear someone will get hurt."

Hannah was devastated. With both Henri and Andrepont at gunpoint she had no choice but to give Weisman the ring.

"Hannah," said Weisman, extending her open palm. "The Seal of Solomon. Give it to me."

Hannah reached into the front pocket of her dress. She removed the ring, looking at it in her hand. She saw the six-pointed star imprinted with the jewels of power. She saw the secret name of God engraved into the band.

This was all wrong. It shouldn't have to be like this.

"Hannah!" said Weisman, more forcefully this time. "The ring! Give it to me now!"

Hannah looked at Henri. She had never seen a face more torn by emotion. This must be the hardest moment of his life, she thought. To see his life's work, the Seal of Solomon, just a few feet away. To be so close, and yet so far away. And to also know Julien's efforts to protect the ring were about to be destroyed.

Henri's eyes met Hannah's, and he slowly shook his head. He mouthed the words, *let it go…*

Hannah glanced once more at the Seal of Solomon. She looked at Professor Weisman and the woman's unbearable grin. Hannah turned to the sea, where the waves crashed at the embankment and sprayed over the railing. She threw the ring as hard as she could.

"No!" cried Weisman lurching at the railing. "You fool! What have you done!"

In the heat of the moment, Andrepont shoved Jurowitz against the car and then knocked him over the head, disarming him with the blow. Henri pinned him down and Andrepont handcuffed him.

Weisman spun around to face Hannah, her face red with rage, her eyes burning. And then her expression changed to a look of shock and confusion. She was staring into a slingshot, aimed directly at her. Slowly, she lifted her hands in the air.

"Do not move," said Clooney, keeping the slingshot leveled. "Do you know who I am?"

Weisman gulped, shaking her head. "I'm sorry. I forget your name."

"I do not look familiar? Not even from the movies?"

She looked entirely confused. "I supposed you do look… a little bit… like a young version of George Clooney?" she ventured.

"That is right. George Clooney," he said. "But my name is Samir Yusef, and I am from Jerusalem."

Just then, Andrepont seized Weisman and handcuffed her, and she slumped in astonishment. Andrepont threw her and Jurowitz into the backseat of the car and then radioed in for assistance.

Hannah ran to her grandfather and threw her arms about his waist, squeezing him hard as she could. "Henri! I was so worried about you. Were you scared?"

"Only for you, my clever little fox," he said, pulling her tighter.

"Did they hurt you?"

"Not in the least," he said. "They needed me alive to help them find the treasure. Or so Weisman thought. Little did they know, you're the real archaeologist of this family." He released his grip and bent to look at her.

His eyes twinkled as he gazed into her own. He appeared to be searching for something, looking first into one eye, then the other, and finally, as though finding what he sought, he nodded with satisfaction and gave her a wink. "Always knew you had it," he said, standing. "It is no small thing, going through this world with an eye like that."

Andrepont rejoined them. He made sure no one was hurt, and assured Hannah that Professor Weisman and Jurowitz would be heading straight to jail.

"And you," he said, addressing Clooney and the slingshot in his hand. "You know it is illegal to carry a slingshot?"

Clooney looked down, biting his lip.

Andrepont said, "Good thing my officer didn't take it from you back at the Temple Mount. I think you saved the day. Well done," he said. "Very well done."

Inspector Andrepont turned the Cancellarii over to the Akko police. Then he drove Henri, Hannah, and Clooney back to Jerusalem, the four of them talking at once, trading stories of their adventures, each demanding to know how the other had figured out this or that.

Andrepont dropped them off before Damascus Gate at the Old City. The three of them thanked the inspector and waved goodbye. They passed beneath the limestone arch of the Old City, Henri and Hannah walking hand-in-hand.

Once inside the Muslim Quarter, Henri took a deep breath, as though inhaling the world. "I love this place," he said. "I love Jerusalem, and I love its mysteries. For that I thank you," he said to Hannah.

"Thank me? But why? You must be heartbroken. I cast your life's work into the sea."

"Did you?" he said. "But don't you see, Hannah? The mystery lives on! For people like us, it's not the answer we seek. It's the journey of discovery, both inside and out. It is the adventure!"

"The adventure," she said, smiling. "That I understand."

"And I must thank you, young man," Henri said to Clooney, clapping a hand upon his shoulder, "for looking after my greatest treasure and keeping her safe in my absence. It appears you did a splendid job."

"It was not easy," said Clooney. "This girl is like a magnet to trouble."

Henri chuckled knowingly, and then halted, looking around. "I have an idea. This way, I want to show you both something."

Henri purchased three tickets at a small booth. He led them up an old staircase attached to the outer wall of the city. When they reached the top, Hannah found she was standing atop Jerusalem's enormous stone wall.

"This path follows the wall around the entire city," said Henri. "We can walk the whole thing and see all of Jerusalem from above. Whenever I'm gone for a time, I like to walk the outer wall. It gives me perspective. There's no view like it in all of Jerusalem."

They strolled together, the three of them. To the left, beyond the wall itself, they could see the hillsides surrounding the Old City and the olive groves in the valley. They paused for a moment to enjoy the view.

Henri put his arm around Hannah. "It is so good to see you, my dear. And to know you've made a true friend," he said. "Clooney, would you take a photo of my granddaughter and I?"

"Let's do all three of us together," said Hannah. She took out her phone and held it out before her. Hannah and Clooney stood side-by-side, Henri just behind, with a hand on each of their shoulders. Just before clicking the shutter, Hannah turned to Clooney and kissed him on the cheek.

"There," she said. "You kept your word, and now I have kept mine."

They looked at the picture on her phone. Clooney's look of surprise was perfectly captured at the very moment of Hannah' kiss.

Clooney stood stunned, touching his cheek. "My very first kiss," he said. "And I even have proof! Hannah, you must send me that photo.

She smiled. "I can do better than that."

Hannah began pressing buttons on her phone. "What are you doing now?" asked Henri.

"Updating my wallpaper."

Henri beamed. "No longer worried you might forget your father?" he asked.

Hannah shook her head. "No. I am not."

"Excellent," said Henri. "Onward and forward then. Next topic of discussion: I have a new expedition in mind. I could certainly use two assistants."

"I'm in!" said Clooney.

"A new expedition? Already?" asked Hannah. "But you just lost your life's work. How can you already have another expedition in mind?"

Henri chuckled. "Hannah, my dear! What made you think Julien Dubuisson stopped hunting for treasures after finding Solomon's ring?"

"You mean… Julien found more?"

Henri winked. "Lots more! I have his second journal to prove it."

"His *second* journal!" said Clooney.

"Of course! Though we may have to find you a passport, young man. Julien journeyed far and wide, and we will have some rough travelling ahead."

"Fine by me," said Clooney. "Where are we off to?"

"*Cambodia*," said Henri. "And you won't believe what we're searching for…"

END

Acknowledgements

Many thanks to Eoin Murray, fellow author and expert on Middle East politics. Your counsel was indispensable. Thanks also to Natasha Deen for your early reading and keen insight—the story is better because of you. Gregg Silver, Bali Panesar, Christiane Panesar, I'll never forget our time together, wandering the labyrinthine lanes of Jerusalem, getting lost, finding wonders—all of which inspired the momentum of this story.

Leala Enfield, you have my heart.

I would also like to acknowledge the superior quality of dark roast coffee over light roast, no matter the trend, for it too has a role in every word I write.

Last of all, I must thank all the folks at Great Plains Publications Ltd for your faith and support. Gregg Shilliday, Catharina de Bakker, Mel Marginet, Irene Bindi, you have my gratitude.